One Lane Bridge

One Lane Bridge

↔

A NOVEL

↔

DON REID

David C Cook
transforming lives together

ONE LANE BRIDGE
Published by David C. Cook
4050 Lee Vance View
Colorado Springs, CO 80918 U.S.A.

David C. Cook Distribution Canada
55 Woodslee Avenue, Paris, Ontario, Canada N3L 3E5

David C. Cook U.K., Kingsway Communications
Eastbourne, East Sussex BN23 6NT, England

David C. Cook and the graphic circle C logo
are registered trademarks of Cook Communications Ministries.

This story is a work of fiction. All characters and events are the product of the author's
imagination. Any resemblance to any person, living or dead, is coincidental.

LCCN 2010932063
ISBN 978-1-4347-6508-6
eISBN 978-0-7814-0576-8

© 2010 Don Reid
Published in association with The Seymour Agency,
475 Miner Street Road, Canton, NY 13617.

The Team: Don Pape, Steve Parolini, Amy Kiechlin,
Sarah Schultz, Caitlyn York, Karen Athen
Cover Design: Gearbox Design, David Carlson
Cover Image: Getty Images, photographer B.SCHMID, rights managed

Printed in the United States of America
First Edition 2010

1 2 3 4 5 6 7 8 9 10

080310

To Debbie:

I'll go to my grave loving you

PART I

Late Summer
2007

Chapter One

J. D. and Karlie Wickman walked down the old marble hall toward the heavy front doors of the police station in silence. This argument had been going on for over a week. They both were of a right mind and a good heart on what needed to be done; the only problem was that there seemed to be more than one right way of doing it. Their two main disagreements in twenty-one years of marriage were about things that had good and logical solutions. How to discipline Angela—that had been the first. Karlie was the disciplinarian while J. D. always let up on the rules. The second? What to spend money on and how much. J. D. tended to see what *had* to be spent while Karlie saw what *needed* to be spent. If the house trim needed to be repainted every five years, then Karlie saw it as a necessity, but if the trim lasted six, J. D. saw it as a savings. Problems of the heart never entered into their disagreements, so they counted themselves lucky and learned to give a little, knowing they would eventually settle on the right solution. They would this time too, but it might take a little longer. That silent walk down the hall suggested they should let the discussion rest a few hours.

But Karlie knew they wouldn't, and the sooner they got it settled, the better. As they walked out the large wooden doors and down the steps toward their car, she fired the first gentle volley.

"I don't think you're being realistic."

"I don't think you're being reasonable," said J. D.

"Do you want to put somebody in prison? Is that your goal here?"

"Yeah, maybe. If that's the punishment for stealing, well, maybe that's where they should be."

"Oh, come on, J. D. You know these women, these girls. You like them. *I* like them. You know we can put a stop to this without having to play cops and robbers like some weekend schoolboys."

The car beeped as J. D unlocked the doors, and they slid into their seats; he in the driver's and she in the passenger's. J. D. stared out the windshield and checked his cell phone messages. Karlie straightened the stacks of receipts littering the floorboard, thinking about the conversation they had just had with their old high school friend, now Sergeant Bobby Caywood of the Hanson Police Department.

Bobby didn't solve their problem and didn't offer his opinion on their opposing solutions. His silence on the matter only added to the tension they were feeling from the daily money shortages.

Karlie could see it in J. D.'s eyes and hear it in his voice. He was concerned not just by the losses but also by how they were going to deal with them—with the apparent theft. Of course she was concerned too, but J. D. always seemed to take business matters more to heart.

When they explained how the money was disappearing from their restaurants, Bobby suggested a couple different routes to take, but she could see he didn't like being a referee.

J. D. set his phone down and looked over at her. "You know, we really put Bobby on the spot in there today."

"Well, he's a policeman. He's used to being on the spot."

"Honey, we can solve this thing ourselves. We've got nearly a thousand dollars missing, and it has to be one of three peo—"

"J. D., let's not go over it again. You just get more upset every time, and I don't want to see you go through that. We'll do it your way. I know you want to try and catch the person responsible."

"And you want to just ask them outright if they're stealing and hope someone'll 'fess up." His face reddened again, and his voice got tighter with each word.

She put her hand on his arm. "J. D, please. Let's go home and tackle this later."

As her husband pulled out into traffic, Karlie looked out her window at the passing shops and signs and tried to remember more pleasant times. Neither she nor J. D. wanted to confront the people and the problem at hand … *but life and business don't always ask permission for the courses they take,* she thought. She watched J. D. out of the corner of her eye all the way home, and it wasn't until they stopped in the driveway that she broke the silence.

"I didn't want to tell you till we got this little episode behind us today, but Angela called this morning."

"What's wrong? She find a shoe store on campus and needs more money?"

She heard his sarcasm but also the humor in his question.

"No, that would be simple." They made eye contact for the first time since getting in the car.

"She sick?"

"No, but she wants to come home." Karlie waited for his reaction.

"She's only been there three weeks. You said yourself she would get homesick and made me promise not to go get her. Have you changed your mind?"

"A girl got attacked in front of the library last night, and Angela's scared to death."

"What do you mean *attacked?*"

"Somebody grabbed her. Ripped her clothes. She got away, and nobody was hurt, but the whole campus is in an uproar."

"Does Angela know the girl?"

"Knows of her—she lives in the next dorm. Angela was crying and pretty upset. Says she wants to come home."

"For good or for the weekend?"

"She says for good. I said for the weekend. She wants you to call her. But before you do, let me say this: Don't give in to her. Don't go racing up there to rescue her. Let her come for the weekend, but please don't let her talk you into anything permanent."

Karlie was never fooled by the tone of her husband's voice or his words where their daughter was concerned. No matter how tough a stand he agreed to take, Karlie knew that Angela always had her daddy's heart firmly in her pocket. She could get what she wanted from him anytime and change her mind as often as she liked, and he would still find a way to see it her way. He'd complain about her being impulsive and irresponsible, but in the end he'd always cave in, excusing her behavior by saying, "But she's young...." Angela was daddy's girl—and *most* of the time, Karlie liked that.

J. D. sat looking at his wife for a moment, apparently waiting for more words from her. He turned off the engine, stared straight ahead again, and said, "You amaze me. You can be harder on your daughter than on an employee."

"Honey, I'm not being hard on anyone. I'm just doing what I think is right."

J. D. took a deep breath and opened the car door. "I'll call her and see if she needs to come home."

Chapter Two

Home was Hanson, North Carolina, and always had been. Hanson wasn't a big town, but it was growing enough that J. D. and Karlie no longer knew most of the merchants on Main Street. The last census had come in around twenty-eight thousand, and with all the industrial growth on the outskirts, the population could easily double in the next decade or two. J. D. and Karlie had both gone to elementary and high school here, then away to college and back. They married in a local church and started a home in the neighbor-hood where they had grown up. Both business majors, they had always shared a dream of opening a restaurant. This dream had come true five years ago, and now there were two restaurants: The Dining Club—Downtown and The Dining Club—West End. Their restaurants kept them busy but happy and, thankfully, successful at the same time. But *happy* was a relative term. The headaches and worry of running a business might bring fulfillment, but as J. D. and Karlie found out, those things could also keep a person's blood pressure at the top of the chart. The recent discovery of money shortages at the downtown site was a situation that brought more headaches than fulfillment.

J. D. was consumed with finding out which waitress was stealing from them and firing her immediately. He had been wrestling with the puzzle for days without relief. But now, for a few moments anyway, he wasn't thinking about the theft. When Angela was on his mind, there was room for little else. His tunnel vision drove him to get her on the phone as quickly as possible so he could listen to the tone of her voice as well as her words. Only then would he know for sure how serious the situation was. He was out of the car and on the sofa, phone in his hand, before the whining and clicking under the hood of his BMW died down.

"Did you reach her?"

"I got her voice mail. She may still be in class. I think she's got a late class on Mondays, doesn't she?"

"I think so," Karlie said. "Wait until later tonight. Give her a little time to get used to it. She has her friends there, and I told her not to go out alone. Let's call her after dinner, and we'll both talk to her and see what's what. Okay?"

"Okay." J. D. agreed because he also needed the extra time to live with it. He stood up, and Karlie came to him and gave him a much-needed hug.

"Did you check *our* machine for calls?" she asked as she reached down and pushed the blinking button.

The machine spoke: "Mr. and Mrs. Wickman, this is Mrs. Rodell. I'm a nurse at Maple Manor, and Mrs. Wickman asked me to call and ask if you are coming to visit tomorrow. Please feel free to call me back at this number. I'll be here until nine."

Karlie looked at him. "I usually erase these messages before you have to hear them. Your mother—she knows we're always there every Tuesday morning, but she gets a nurse to call every Monday after-noon with the same message."

"Well, great. What else do you think is going to happen today?"

"I don't know. But I tell you what, let's eat here, go by and check the restaurants, and then call it a day."

"Twist my arm, please. Twist my arm."

"I'll do better than that. How about I close up both restaurants tonight, and you put the top down and go driving in the country?"

This was a generous offer J. D. couldn't refuse. It was his favor-ite thing to do on a late summer evening when the sun had given up on the day and was dying its slow and sure death. No matter how bad the day had been, he could always go to the garage and pull out his little green Triumph (which had seen better days and even better years), rev it up, and head for a country road. Getting lost was half the fun—and letting the wind hit him in the face was the other half. It blew away the dust that had gathered since the last ride and prepared him for whatever the morrow held. He would talk to Angela later tonight, see his mother come morning, and decide on how to handle the money problem at the downtown restaurant before closing time tomorrow. But for now he wasn't going to think about anything but that ride in the country. He thanked Karlie with a kiss.

→

Route 724 was a typical country road just wide enough for two cars
to meet comfortably but not wide enough to pass a slow driver safely.
J. D. would pull to the side whenever a restless driver got behind
him and let them go by on their merry way. He could always sense a
driver's schedule or lack thereof by their speed and how closely they
rode his bumper. When J. D. was on one of these head-clearing little
drives, he was always the slowest vehicle on the road. He had no
place in particular to go and no set time to get there. He was simply
enjoying the sights, the smells, and feel of the country.

It must have been about 7:20 p.m., the sun just losing its early
September strength, when he rounded a curve and saw a sign that
read One Lane Bridge. He slowed as he looked across to make sure
no one was entering from the other side, then stopped in the middle
of the bridge to listen to the small river that ran under it. Weeping
willows lined either side of the small, quaint stream, which was about
twenty feet wide from bank to bank—and beyond the willows, he
saw nothing but beautiful pastures. Just the sight of it brought tran-
quility he hadn't felt for days. He was tempted to pull over, take off
his shoes, roll up his pants, and wade in up to his knees. The thought
of doing this brought a smile to his face, and he shivered and shook
his head to snap out of the notion. He drove at a creeping pace across
the rest of the bridge, drinking in the peace he could feel all around
him.

Then, just as he was going down the grade from the bridge, he
smelled heat from his engine. He inspected his gauges, and, sure

enough, his Triumph had overheated. He immediately pulled to the side of the road, got out, and opened the hood. The smell of antifreeze and a small stream of steam rose from the radiator. He was in the middle of nowhere with nowhere to go for help. His first thought was to call Karlie or his friend Jack. But his very next thought was one of panic when he realized he might not be able to tell them exactly where he was. Was he still on Route 724? Did he take a right at that barn a few miles back and maybe a left at the last crossroads? He wasn't sure. He could always backtrack to get home, but he wasn't certain he could give anyone directions on how to find him. He snapped his cell phone from his belt and flipped it open. He was getting zero reception. He dialed Karlie's number twice, but nothing happened. He walked twenty yards both ways, hoping to find a signal, but still nothing. The sun was a little dimmer, and he was a little more lost than he had been ten minutes before. Certainly someone would come along, and he could hitch a ride back to town. He waited fifteen, then twenty minutes and was beginning to feel more stressed with each tick of the watch. Not one car came in sight.

He scanned the horizon and didn't even see any houses. But he did see some cows. *Where there are cows, there have to be people not far away,* he thought. He noticed a dirt lane a few paces behind the car. As he walked up the path, he spotted a chimney behind a grassy hill. There *was* a house—and it wasn't far at all. He began to walk up the lane and could see the house growing bigger and closer with each step.

It was an old farmhouse—weatherboard in need of paint, two chimneys, badly patched roof, small front porch with a swing, and, thankfully, no barking dog in the yard. The picket fence partially surrounding the house was falling down and missing a gate, and the sheds out back were in an even worse state of repair. But the chickens in the yard told him someone was obviously living here, and that was exactly what he needed: someone who could give him a bucket of water or let him use a phone to call for help.

He walked through the opening where the gate once was and across a dirt yard to the two steps leading up to the front porch. There he found a screen door with no screen and an ornate solid wood door with a window in the top half. The glass was cracked from corner to corner. He opened the shell of the screen door and knocked three times. The window rattled as if it might fall out with a fourth knock. When no one answered, he walked around the house, side-stepping a few chickens, and knocked at what was clearly the kitchen door. Having no more luck there, he stepped back and looked at the second-story windows before yelling, "Is anyone home?"

There was no car in the back, and he heard no reply, but he took his chances and yelled again, "Hello! Hello! Anybody here?"

His call was answered by footsteps on gravel behind him. "Yes sir. Can I help you?"

Startled, J. D. turned around quickly and said, "Ah—hi."

"Hi yourself. Can I help you?"

The man staring back at him was tall and thin, wearing work jeans and a heavy chambray shirt. He was carrying a bucket. His back was bent just enough to tell J. D. he was well familiar with hard work—and his weathered skin suggested he was used to doing that hard work in the sun and the wind. He wore a tan cap, stained around the edges from the sweat of his labor and plain in front where there might typically be some sort of advertising. He wore work shoes with soles and heels worn thin and the tops caked with dust. The man, in his early fifties or so, had a pleasant yet sad air about him.

"I'm afraid I'm lost. My car overheated down here in front of your drive. I was wondering if you could give me a hand."

"I'll do what I can. I ain't much of a mechanic."

"Oh, I don't need much. I just need a bucket of water."

"Well, that I can help you with. Would you like to come in?"

"Thanks," J. D. said and followed the man through the back door into the small and rustic kitchen.

"I'll draw you a bucket of water. Can I offer you some coffee or anything?" the man asked as he washed his hands at the kitchen sink.

"No, thanks. I would like to use your phone, though, to call my wife and let her know where I am."

"Can't help you there, son. We don't have a telephone."

"No phone?"

"Naw," he said, drying his hands on a threadbare towel hanging from a wall hook. "We go across the hill to the next farm when we have to make a call. I can walk you over there if you want."

"No, that's fine. It's not that important."

The man was about to say something when he was interrupted by a voice from somewhere farther back in the house. "Paul. Paul! Who is it?"

"That's my wife," the farmer—Paul, as J. D. was putting all this together—explained. "She's bedridden." Then he raised his voice and answered back, "A visitor, Ada. A man with car trouble." He looked at J. D. and said, "She's sick. We've made her a bed in the parlor. She don't go out anymore. Maybe never will."

"Who is it, Paul?" the voice called again.

Paul looked at J. D. and asked, "Who do I tell her it is? You got a name?"

"John David Wickman," he said, not sure why he was being so formal with his answer.

Paul hollered back, "His name is John. He's from town, and he needs water for his automobile."

"Tell him to come in. I never get to see anybody anymore."

"She's sick, but she's also lonesome. Nobody much comes around. Would you like to go in and see her?"

J. D. said, "Sure, I'll go in and see her," and followed Paul through hanging beads in a doorway that opened into a modest dining room and then through a wider doorway that became the living room or parlor. All the shades were pulled, and J. D. could just barely make out the shape of a couple of chairs, a sofa, and, over near the front door, a daybed with a figure lying on it. He assumed this was Ada, Paul's wife. As he came closer he could see the outline of a frail, small body. Her skin was pale and yellowed, and her hair was long and stringy and matted around her forehead. He could smell sickness in the room, and the air became difficult to breathe. Ada reached out her hand and said in a weak voice, "I heard you knock. What's your name again?"

"John," J. D. said. He was surprised at how foreign his given name sounded rolling off his tongue. Only a few teachers in high school had ever called him that.

"John. Sit down, John. There's a chair right there."

J. D. stumbled in the near-dark room and felt a straight chair behind him. He sat down while Paul stood in the center of the room. J. D. picked up the conversation to fill the awkward silence.

"I had a little car trouble, and your husband is helping me out. I appreciate your hospitality."

"Paul will help you. He's good help. He's a good man. He keeps me alive every day."

"I see. And your name is Ada? Is that right?"

"Ada Clem. And this is my husband, Paul. Have you met him?"

As J. D. was answering, "Yes, ma'am, I have," Paul interjected, "She forgets. Sometimes right in the middle of a thought. She knows you one minute, and the next she don't."

"I see," J. D. repeated nervously. "Well, Mrs. Clem, I guess I better start back to town. I'll get your husband to give me a hand, and I'll be on my way."

Ada held out her arm from her bed again as if reaching for something. J. D.'s first instinct was to step toward her and shake her hand, but then on closer inspection it looked as if even a gentle squeeze could break every fragile bone. She peered up at him with watery eyes and said in a faltering voice, "Will you get me something in town, John?"

"Sure. If I can."

"Would you get me a Dixie Cup of ice cream? I love store-bought ice cream. You know what I mean in a Dixie Cup?"

"Yes ma'am, I know."

"Ada." Paul spoke gently and firmly. "This gentleman ain't comin' back out here. He's just passing by."

"Well, he'll have to come back to bring me my Dixie Cup, won't he?"

"We gotta go now, Ada. This man has to get home for supper."

Maybe it was the word *supper* that turned J. D.'s attention to the smell of something frying in the kitchen, or maybe it was the smell itself that caused him to look toward the doorway with the hanging colored beads. Either way, it was the tension breaker that gave him the opportunity to stand and say, "Good evening, Mrs. Clem. It was nice to meet you, and I hope you're feeling better soon."

The feeble voice from the daybed in the ever-growing darkness said, "Good-bye, sir. It was good making your acquaintance."

Paul led the way, this time toward the kitchen and the good smell of something simmering on the stove. As J. D. pushed through the beads, he could just barely hear music, apparently coming from a radio. But the sight that stopped him was of someone standing at the stove, flipping bread with a spatula into a skillet. The "someone" was small and female, and from the back he couldn't determine her age. Her hair was long and pulled straight back from her head. She was wearing a thin, light-green dress and was humming with the music from the radio as if unaware of anyone else in the house.

"John, this is my daughter, Lizzie. Lizzie, honey, this is Mr. Wickerman."

"Wickman," J. D. corrected as Lizzie turned around and said, "Hi."

J. D. estimated this pretty young girl to be fourteen years old, but her eyes looked so much older. And although she seemed friendly and bright, he was at a loss as to what else to say to her. His head was still spinning from the conversation he'd just had with her mother.

"John, would you like to stay for supper?" Paul asked.

"Oh, no, I couldn't. I just ate before I left home. And I really do need to get back. My wife will be wondering where I am."

Lizzie spoke over her shoulder. "We ain't got much. We're having fried bread and applesauce. You like fried bread?"

"Ah, sure. But I'm not hungry, really."

"Is that your car down on the road?" Lizzie asked, then added before he had time to answer, "It sure is a pretty one."

"Thank you."

"Can I go for a ride sometime?"

"Lizzie, Mr. Wickerman is just passing by. He don't have time for that."

J. D. fumbled again for the right parting word. "It was good to meet you, Lizzie. I hope to see you again sometime."

"John, you wait here while I draw that bucket of water, and then I'll walk down with you to your car."

As the back door closed, J. D. and Lizzie were left in the room alone. He didn't know what to say to a fourteen-year-old, so he decided to say nothing. But as she shoveled more butter-battered bread into the skillet, she broke the silence for him.

"Did you come out here to see my mamma?"

"No, I...."

"'Cause if you did, I don't want you gettin' her hopes up if you really can't help her. We've had other people out here who claimed they could help her and never did. She just gets sicker, and my daddy gets sadder. So if you're one of those ..."

Her words trailed off with the sizzling from the stovetop. He could hear tears in her voice—but more than that, anger.

"Who tried to help her, Lizzie? Doctors?"

"No. Not real doctors. But medicine people. People who have all kinds of cures that never work."

There were so many things to ask, but he sensed the girl was upset over things she didn't really understand. He didn't want to push buttons she didn't have the maturity to handle. He nearly asked, "What are you cooking?" before remembering she'd already told him.

J. D. could only imagine that Lizzie was frying bread because there was nothing else in the house for supper. The words stumbled awkwardly out of his mouth.

"Lizzie, I, ah … I own a restaurant. We … we have lots of food there …"

"We've got food, Mr. Wickerman. That's what I'm doing now is fixing supper."

"But if there's anything you need … I mean … if you need something …"

"We're doing fine, Mr. Wickerman. Me and Daddy and Mamma, we like fried bread."

The door opened, and Paul stuck his head in and said, "Got your water, John. Let's go get this contraption started."

John turned and started toward the door. Lizzie had her back to him, intent on what she was doing at the stove. J. D. recognized the music on the radio—traditional country music. Ernest Tubb or Eddy Arnold or one of those older guys. The sweet smell of bread warmed the chilly, twilight-tinged kitchen. He decided against saying good-bye to the girl, wondering if he'd offended her. He quietly slipped through the back door and out into the dirt yard, following Paul, who was a good twenty yards ahead of him with a two-gallon bucket of water in his hand.

As they approached the green TR3, Paul whistled and said,

"Wow. Now that's a dandy-lookin' machine. Never seen one of those. What do you call it?"

"Triumph. English made. Little banged up. Needs a little work, but it runs pretty good."

"Well, here, I'll let you put the water in. I might pour it in the wrong hole."

They laughed, and J. D. got in the driver's seat and started the engine just in case it hadn't cooled down enough. He remembered all too well the first car he ever had while still in high school. This same thing had happened to him and his friend Jack. They had pulled into a service station and got a water hose—and in their youthful ignorance, filled the steaming radiator with the motor off and busted the block in the engine. His father never got over it. So while J. D. filled the radiator, this time with the motor purring, Paul stood off to the side, watching intently with his hands in his pockets. J. D. spoke to him without turning.

"Mr. Clem, has a doctor seen your wife?"

"Doctors cost a lot of money, son. And I don't know what they can do for her."

"Well, I don't either. But shouldn't someone see her?"

"There's been folks here to see her, but nobody can help."

J. D. turned and looked the farmer in the face and saw the fear in his eyes. "Paul, I'll pay for a doctor if you'll let me bring one out. And do you need food?"

Paul Clem's face froze, and his eyes went from sad to indignant. J. D. knew he had crossed the line, but it was too late to retract his words.

"We're doin' just fine, Mr. Wickerman. We have food on the

table, and we don't need any doctor. I ain't on relief and never have been. Good day, sir, and it was pleasant meetin' you."

"Mr. Clem, I'm sorry if I offended you. I never meant to imply that you were not a good provider. I just thought … I just wanted you to know that I was willing to help in any way I could."

Halfway through his last sentence, he found himself talking to the back of a figure walking slowly but determinedly up the dirt lane toward the rundown farmhouse. And as J. D. stood swallowing bitter words he wished he had never spoken, he looked farther up the hill and saw the silhouette of Lizzie Clem against the nearly nighttime sky. She was waiting for her daddy to come to supper.

J. D. slammed the hood, then the car door, and turned the Triumph sharply around in the road to head back across the one lane bridge toward town. He now had his daughter, his mother, his business, and a family of strangers vying for time and space in his overworked and troubled conscience. He hadn't prayed in years and wasn't real sure he still remembered how. But he felt an overwhelming need for some sort of spiritual comfort … or maybe he was just tired. Getting these people named Clem off his mind was not going to be easy.

Chapter Three

It was after nine when J. D. got home. Karlie was in the den with cotton stuffed between each toe, painting her nails and watching TV. She didn't look up when he sat down heavily in his chair next to her.

"Angela called," she said. "She's fine. I told her we wouldn't call anymore tonight and if she still wanted to, we'd come get her for the weekend. But she's doing much better. Said to tell you hi."

J. D. listened but didn't react. He was glad that things were better and glad not to have to talk to her tonight. He didn't want to talk to anyone. His mind was full of a family he had left somewhere out past 724 just beyond the one lane bridge. They were hungry and one was sick and at least one was offended and maybe two of them angry. He had made a mess of trying to help, and he was feeling guiltier by the minute. He suspected Karlie could sense his uneasiness, and his suspicions were confirmed when she asked, "What's wrong?"

His first instinct was to say, "Nothing. I'm just tired," but he thought of how irritated he became when she would say that to him, so he decided to tell her what had happened while he was out for his "peaceful" ride in the country. When he finished, she looked at him with those eyes that always understood exactly what he was feeling. And then she offered the perfect solution.

"Go to bed. Get some rest. And tomorrow after we go see your mother, we'll take some groceries out, and if the old man gets mad, he'll just have to get over it."

J. D., finding no fault with that decision, smiled in agreement. Then he picked up the newspaper from the end table by the sofa and headed upstairs. If only going to sleep were as easy as climbing into bed, he would have found the relief he so needed. At 3:00 a.m. he was still staring at the shadows on the wall and the lights from the street. None of the thoughts would settle down in his mind. They kept fighting for position in his line of worry. Angela, in a strange city with strange people, and frightened. His mother, living in less-than-desirable surroundings in a nursing home that did its best to make her comfortable but couldn't begin to feel like home. Someone stealing from them at the restaurant almost daily. And those poor people, the Clems, living in squalor with sickness and death in the next room, eating what was available and cheap and enjoying barely the necessities of life.

He didn't deserve to sleep.

→

Karlie was dressed when J. D. finally opened his eyes. As she was going out the bedroom door, she said, "I'm going to stop in at the restaurant downtown for just a few minutes. See how everything is going. Let's decide before the day is over if we want to confront them or if we want to plant the bills tonight in the cashbox. I will be okay with whatever we decide."

J. D. had to smile at her sincerity. "Me, too," he said. "Then where are you going?"

"I'll meet you at Maple Manor at ten o'clock. We'll have coffee with your mother, and then we'll stop by Kroger and get some food and head out to the country. Is that still what you want to do?"

"Yeah."

"Say so if it's not. Have you changed your mind?"

"No."

"Something's up. What is it?"

"Let's switch the order around. Let's take the groceries out there first and then go see Mom."

"Okay by me, but she'll call a dozen times, you know."

"She'll be all right. I just need to get this thing off my mind. Meet me at Kroger at ten."

"You're the boss," she said as she bent over the bed and kissed him good-bye.

He could smell the coffee she had brewing for him in the kitchen. He could see the sun pushing past the open curtains at each bedroom window. But he couldn't feel the shower spray hitting him in the face, and if he didn't feel that pretty soon, he might still be lying there at noon. He threw the covers back and jumped to his feet. He had to shake yesterday from his head in order to face today.

$$\rightarrow$$

Karlie's van was filled with plastic bags of every kind of food imaginable. They had bought bread and milk and sugar and salt and flour and all kinds of meat—things that every household needs. But they had also filled other bags with candy and a cake and a couple of pies and potato chips and pretzels and Cokes. And, of course, he had Ada's ice cream. He couldn't find any Dixie Cups, but he found individual servings in plastic cups that would have to suffice.

They drove mostly in silence, but after a few twists and turns, Karlie began to tease him.

"How did you ever get on this road?"

"I told you. I just drive till I get lost."

"Well, you've certainly got me lost, big boy. I have no idea where I am. Had you ever been on this road before?"

"I don't think so. I try to find a new one every time I take one of those mind-clearing excursions. And this time, I think I outdid myself."

Karlie looked at him and laughed. "I don't mean to sound like a kid on vacation, but how much farther is it?"

"If memory serves, we're about there. Just around that next bend is the one lane bridge, and then just over the bridge is the lane that goes up to the ..."

His words trailed off about the same time their van came to a slow stop in the middle of the road.

"What's wrong, honey? You know you've stopped in the middle of the road, right?"

J. D. was staring straight ahead in a sudden empty stupor. His mind was trying to find reason and rationale, but the blood rushing in his head was rendering him unable to think.

"J. D., what's wrong? Are you all right?"

He pointed a good fifteen seconds before he finally spoke, and what he said sent chills up Karlie's spine and neck.

"Karlie, the one lane bridge is gone."

"What?"

"The one lane bridge. It's not here."

"Maybe it's down the road a little ways."

"No. It was here. Right here where this two lane bridge is. Except when it was a one lane bridge it had high steel sides and cables running from the top of it down into the ground. This isn't the same bridge. I mean, the bridge I drove over ... it was one of those bridges where you'd have to sit and wait if someone was crossing from the other side. The steel bridge is gone, and it's two lanes now."

"J. D., it has to be on down the road. You've only been here once before. You can't possibly know the road this well."

"Believe me, I know it. The bridge is gone."

"Honey, you're scaring me. Now stop it. And look at you. You're shaking."

J. D. got out of the car and walked to the bridge. Karlie followed him. They stood in silence by the cement siding that braced the two lane bridge. He stared below at the river while she stared at him. She was about to speak when they both had to jump back from a truck that whizzed by, horn blaring.

"J. D., be reasonable. That bridge did not disappear overnight. We are either on the wrong road or it's farther on. A bridge can't get up and move."

He stood for a long time looking across the shallow water and then brought his gaze back to meet hers. "Okay. You drive. We'll keep going a bit. But I'm sure this is where it was."

Karlie drove while J. D. stared out the passenger window. She had driven for another five miles when he finally said, "Turn around here. There's no sense in going any farther."

Karlie turned into the pull-off area, but instead of turning around in the road, she stopped and turned off the engine. She looked at her husband, who was still staring out the windshield.

"J. D., something is seriously wrong here. You have been under a lot of stress with everything that's going on. Now either you admit we might be on the wrong road, or when we get back to town we are going to see a doctor and get you some rest. You have to know all this is not normal."

"We're not on the wrong road, Karlie. Turn around, and I'll show you where the house is. Or was."

She did as requested, and as the two-lane-bridge crossing came into sight, J. D. said, "Pull in here."

He pointed to a country convenience store on the left that they had passed a few minutes earlier coming the other way. She stopped next to the front door and sat in the car as J. D. got out and went inside. A bell dinged when he opened the front door, and a heavyset man in his mid-forties reached over and turned down a television set behind the counter. He said, "Mornin'."

"Good morning. I'm lost—I'm wondering if you could help me."

"Do what I can."

"I'm looking for a family by the name of Clem that lives out here somewhere. I thought they lived right along here, about where this store is."

"Clems. I don't know any Clems. There's some Clements that live down the road a piece. But Clems. I don't think I know any."

"Well, can you tell me this?" J. D. asked with all the strength he could muster. "How long has this store been here?"

"Oh, man, I don't know. I bought it about fifteen years ago when I moved from Wisconsin. But the store was here years before."

J. D.'s voice and legs were getting weaker, but he still had to ask, "Do you know of any one lane bridges around here?"

"One lane bridges." The big man frowned as he looked out over the rims of his glasses. "You mean one of those covered wooden bridges?"

"No, no. One of those big steel ones with the twenty-foot sides on it and the steel cables and all."

"Naw," he shook his head. "Never saw anything like that. Not since I been here."

"You're sure about that?"

"I'm pretty sure I would remember if I'd seen one. What are you a photographer or something? Looking for old bridges?"

"Yeah, something like that. Well, thanks. Sorry to have bothered you."

Karlie was waiting in the car with the same concerned look on her face as when he had left. "Well?" she said.

"The house was just beyond where this store is. I know you think I'm crazy, but it was there, and the bridge was right where that new bridge is."

"J. D., let's go home. Let's just forget about it and go home."

"Wait a minute," he said, much too quickly and way too loudly. He pulled out his cell phone, opened it, and stared down at the bars looking back at him. He looked at his wife and said, "We have service."

"Was there some reason you thought we wouldn't?"

J. D. snapped his cell phone shut and put it back on his belt. He laid his head back against the headrest, closed his eyes, and with a sigh said, "Yeah, let's go home. We have ice cream that's melting."

Chapter Four

They drove the eighteen miles back to Hanson in total silence. Neither one of them even turned the radio on. Karlie knew J. D. was expecting her to weigh in on the situation every second of the trip, and she had her mouth open and ready to say something a dozen times but just couldn't think of the right thing to say. She didn't want to aggravate him with her concerns, but she was full of worry over what must have been going on in his mind. She kept watching him out of the corner of her eye and observed he was staring at instead of simply watching the road. She was helpless to know where to begin. So nothing was said until they pulled up in front of Maple Manor.

Karlie spoke first. "Are you up to this?"

"No, but let's do it anyway."

"J. D., you have to admit that everything that is happening is not normal. You've been having headaches in the past month like you've never had before. And I know this restaurant problem has your blood pressure sky-high. You take everything so hard and so serious. And now all this with Angela. I worry about you."

"Well, don't. I'm okay."

"You're *not* okay. Even *you* don't believe that. If you did, you'd be able to explain all these things that are happening."

"Karlie, don't make everything worse than it is. I'm all right now, and I'll be all right later. Can we just leave it at that?"

She heard this as more of a demand than a question and knew she would be challenging him if she continued.

"No, we can't." She was firm, angry, and scared all at the same time.

"So what do you suggest I do?"

"We'll visit for a little while with your mother, and then I want you to promise me you'll make an appointment this afternoon to go see Dr. Maxton."

J. D. looked at her, incredulous. "He's a GP. What's he going to tell me? That I've got the flu or something?"

"Don't be silly. Tell him about all the stress you're under, and maybe he can recommend another doctor. Or maybe he can give you something. I don't know. Just go to him and talk to him."

"All right. I'll go to our family doctor and tell him my wife thinks I'm a nut job. That I've been seeing people and houses that aren't there, and maybe would he please take my blood pressure and give me some aspirin. That ought to do it."

"Be as cynical as you like, but you have to start someplace."

Karlie saw his shoulders relax for the first time that day. And when he spoke, she could hear in the softness of his voice that he was trying to reassure her.

"Honey, I know you mean well. And I would be just as worried about you if the tables were turned. I have no answers right now. But let's go in and see Mom, and then we'll go by the restaurants...."

"And then to the doctor?"

"We'll see. And get the ice cream out of one of those bags back there. We'll take it to Mom."

→

J. D. realized that no matter how many faux antebellum columns were put up in front of a brick building, it was still hard to make a nursing home look warm and fuzzy. And once the front door was opened, it was nearly impossible. The smells that filled his nostrils every time, the sights that invaded his vision no matter how hard he tried not to look, and the sounds that he willed himself to ignore were always the same. He looked straight ahead and walked to his destination in hopes of finding the object of his journey in a good frame of mind and body. And since that object was Beatrice McKinley Wickman, this was usually very possible.

Bea Wickman was eighty-four years old and of extremely sound mind. It was her body that had let her down. She needed round-the-clock attention and found in Maple Manor the home she was looking for. She paid for it herself, and her every decision was still hers alone. She did not dread waking there every morning. She rather enjoyed it. She had a private room, a TV and radio, a sitting area, meals delivered to her quarters three times a day, and even some old friends down the hall who visited and played Hearts every afternoon. J. D. knew that, from her point of view, life could be so much worse. Her biggest problem was convincing her offspring of this. J. D.'s two sisters, Alice and Becky, had tried for years to get her to move closer to them in Kentucky and Virginia so they could look after her, but leaving Hanson was never a consideration for her. J. D. knew that his mother was aware of the undue pressure this put on him, since he still lived in town and felt even more guilt seeing her so often in this environment. Although she had preached to him all his life, "It's the eyes with which you view that make a scene beautiful or not," she couldn't convince him she was happy and satisfied with her home at Maple Manor. She didn't miss a thing—she knew these visits were harder on him each week, and likely sensed that today he seemed more distant than ever. And she surely noticed that even sweet, considerate Karlie did too.

J. D. set his coffee cup on the table by the brown recliner. "Mom, we can't stay long. We've got a mess at one of the restaurants, and we're heading over there right now."

"That's quite all right. I understand. What's the problem?"

J. D. and Karlie looked at one another, smiled, and sighed.

Karlie spoke first, "One of the employees is stealing money from us."

"Oh my goodness." Beatrice's eyes were the shape of a full moon and almost as big. Most people, upon hearing that an employee was stealing money would have said, "Who is it?" or "How much have they stolen?" or maybe even "Have you caught them yet?" But Beatrice asked, "Do they know that you know yet?"

Her question took all the tension out of J. D. and Karlie for a moment as they laughed at her off-center way of thinking, which incidentally had nothing to do with her age or condition. It was her chosen way of seeing life—with a different slant from anyone else.

J. D. answered, "Not yet."

Beatrice leaned closer and lowered her voice and looked toward the open door that led to the hallway. "Be careful. Once they know that you know, they may come and stab you in your sleep. That happened to a friend I went to school with. She caught someone stealing from her, and she confronted him before she went to the police, and he stabbed her in her sleep."

J. D. always knew when it was time to wash up the coffee cups in her little sink in the corner and begin the good-byeing process. And this was the time.

$$\rightarrow$$

Back in the car, Karlie took charge. "Let's go by the Club—downtown; I'll call Dr. Maxton's nurse, and then you slip over there and talk to him."

The lack of response told her immediately it wasn't going to be that simple. J. D. backed out of the parking lot in silence. She watched him drive intently through town without speaking a word and thought how unlike him it was to be this inward about anything. He always opened up to her with the little things that bothered him, but this was not a little thing. This was something strange and unwanted, and she was getting more frightened by the minute.

"J. D., whatever you're going to do or not going to do, talk to me. That's all I ask. Just talk to me. I want to help."

"I know that. I'm sorry if I'm acting weird, but I'm going to be fine. I'll figure it out. But here's what you can do. You go to the restaurant and check the receipts. Confront whomever you want about whether they're stealing from us or not. I'll concede to you on that one. We'll do it your way. Then let me do *this* my way. I'm not going to see Dr. Maxton. I've got a couple of errands to run and a few other things to do. Just let me do them and give me a little room. That's how you can help."

He pulled the car to the curb in front of the Dining Club Restaurant. Karlie got out, and J. D. drove off.

$$\rightarrow$$

Before parking in the public lot behind the courthouse, J. D. dialed Angela's number on his cell phone. Just hearing her voice and getting reassurance that everything was all right would bring him a step closer to restoring his heartbeat to normal. Then he could focus on what his procedure should be inside the records room under the old courthouse. But the constant ring and eventual sound of Angela's voice greeting told him he wasn't going to feel that relief until some-time later in the day.

The girl behind the desk was young and pretty, her bright eyes suggesting that she just might know what she was doing.

"Hi. My name is J. D. Wickman, and I'm looking for some his-torical land deeds on a particular country road. What information do I need to have?"

The girl, just a few years older than Angela, he guessed, went to the computer and said, "Come on back, Mr. Wickman, and we'll start searching maps on the screen till we find what you want."

He walked through the swinging gate to the girl's desk, which was next to a set of windows looking up into an alley full of air-conditioning units that served the two-century-old building. He rubbed his eyes while she clicked on icons and pulled up the needed programs.

After about a minute, she said, "Okay, do you have an address?"

"No, I don't. I have a route number."

"Okay. What's that?"

"Route 814. It's a state road. It turns off of 724."

"Alrighty. Then what's the name of the landowner?"

"That's what I'm trying to find out."

The girl looked at him, trying to mask her apparent disbelief. With a practiced smile she said, "If you need to look up a historical deed, we need to have the address or the name of the current owner of the property."

"I don't have any of that. I just know it's about fifteen miles or so out that road going south, on the right just past a bridge."

"I'm sorry, sir. But that's not enough information ..."

"Wait a minute. There's a store there now. A country convenience store. It's probably in the phone book, but then we'll still need a name, won't we?"

"Afraid so. Wait … maybe not. Is that the road that comes out in New Park?"

"I don't know. I've never gone all the way through on that road."

The girl smiled and lowered her voice. "I used to date a guy who lived in New Park, and I think I know that back road. Just a minute."

She picked up the phone, buzzed someone in another part of the building, and said, "Ellen, don't you live out in the New Park area? I thought so. Do you know of a convenience store that's between here and there on Route 814?" She held her hand over the mouthpiece and said to J. D., "It's not a Subway shop, is it?"

J. D. shook his head.

"No," the girl said back into the phone. "It's not Subway. A *convenience* store," she emphasized and rolled her eyes at J. D., still smiling. She sat listening to Ellen for what seemed like minutes to J. D., and he watched her facial expressions change from a frown to raised eyebrows to chuckles and wondered if maybe they had started talking about something besides the business at hand. But then suddenly she put her hand over the mouthpiece again and said, "How about Stan's One Stop? A real big guy. He never comes out from behind the counter."

"That's it!" J. D. said much too loudly. "That's him. Stan."

"Thanks, Ellen. See you. Okay," she said, hanging up the phone and looking at J. D. "Now we've got something to go on. Ellen said his name is Stanley Wilshaw. So let's look him up, and we'll find the lot—and then we can search it."

J. D. watched her work through the grids and maps and lot numbers that kept popping up on her computer screen. She typed letters in, deleted others, and added more reference numbers with the skill and flourish of a swordsman on the deck of a pirate ship. She never paused or glanced up until she said, "Got you something. Wilshaw bought the store in September of '92. He bought it from a man named Noah Allmarode. Know him?"

J. D. told her he didn't.

Studying intently as she scrolled, the girl continued, "Allmarode bought the land in 1947 for nine hundred dollars from Lavern Justice. Mmm. Any of this ringing any bells for you?"

"Nothing," J. D. said honestly. "I really don't expect to know any of these people. I'm just trying to find out when the store was built and if there was ever a house out there."

"Oh, I think I can help you there. Looks like the store was built by Allmarode in … let's see. Yes, here it is. Improved property with a commercial building in June of 1964."

"And before that? Still no house?"

The girl's sigh hinted at her growing impatience, or maybe it expressed her increased interest in the thrill of bringing old facts to the present. She *did* work in the courthouse records room. Maybe she loved it. Or maybe she was just biding her time until she got married and started that dream family. J. D. decided not to worry about it as long as she found what he was looking for. What he was looking for was an old two-story frame house. And the reason he was looking for this was … the reason was … he wasn't really sure what the reason was. What would finding a house prove, anyway?

"Here's the house, Mr. Wickman! You are Mr. Wickman who owns the Dining Club restaurants, aren't you?" She continued as J. D. nodded his head, "My dad knows you. Tinker Knicely? You remember him. I think you went to school together."

J. D. remembered him—and remembered he cared little for Tinker in high school and didn't want to get sidetracked on another subject at this particular moment. He just wanted to get back to … "The house. You found something?"

"Yes, it looks like all that land was owned at one time by Carmine Justice. I've heard his name around the courthouse for years. They tell all kinds of stories around here about him. I know you've heard of him. He was a lawyer or a state senator or something. He owned everything on that side of the road for miles at one time, and then in 1945 he died, and his family later split it all up in lots and sold off farm and grazing land."

"Yeah, I've heard of him, but what about the house? Does it say anything in there about a house ever being on the property?"

Tinker Knicely's patient daughter stared at her screen for at least two minutes without saying a word. Then, "There were some rental houses on that plot of land, and it looks as if they were torn down in 1946 when the family began to divide it all up."

"Does it say who the family was … or is?"

"Mr. Carmine had two sons and one daughter. You want the daughter's address?"

"What? That would be a 1946 address wouldn't it?"

"Yes, in the computer listing here it would be. But I can tell you where she lives today. She used to work upstairs in the file room until about six months ago. She retired. I'm not supposed to give out this information, but she doesn't work here anymore so I guess it'll be okay. You know where Belmont Avenue is, don't you? Well, go to the end. Last house on the left."

J. D. was almost to the doorway when he turned back. Ms. Knicely, or whatever her name was, was just getting up from her desk when he said, "One more thing. What about the bridge? Do you have listings for bridges, when they were built, what kind?"

"Not here. State highway department. I can give you a number."

"That's okay. I can find it. Thanks for your help. And give your father my best."

Chapter Five

H ello."
    "Daddy?"

"Hi, baby."

"Have I called you at a bad time?"

"No, not at all. I'm downtown, just getting in the car."

"Is Mamma with you?"

"No, I'm all by myself. Are you all right?"

"I'm fine. Well, better anyway. I guess Mamma told you what happened. It was really scary. The girl it happened to lives just over in West Hall. I can see her room from my window. She's from Illinois, and she's pretty much destroyed over the whole thing. I think she may even be leaving school for good. That's the rumor anyway."

"Are you scared? And Angela, tell me the truth." Ever since she was a little girl, she had tried to be brave beyond her years. She fooled most of her teachers, and her mother, too, with that false-security air, but there wasn't much about his little girl that got past J. D. He knew when she was covering up her deepest feelings. When she was trying to convince him everything was all right, he could always see in her eyes when it wasn't. On the phone, he didn't have the benefit of looking into the honest blue depths of her eyes; he only had her voice, and he wanted to be sure not to misread anything that might be bothering her.

"Not as bad as I was. There's all kinds of security around now that wasn't here two days ago. They've added extra guards, and the town police are riding through every hour. It's not all that bad."

"You still want to come home this weekend?"

"Well, that's why I was calling. I told Mamma I did, but now I don't. I don't mean ever—just that I don't want to come *this* weekend. Does that make sense?"

"Ah, well … sure. You feel better about the safety issue up there, and you're comfortable staying on campus?"

"Yeah, well, sorta, yes."

"Okay, honey. Give it all to me in one sentence. What's up?" This was one of those times he had to throw his parental instincts to the wind and demand, point blank, her honesty. This wasn't an issue of integrity—just evidence of a youthful tendency to live for the moment.

"They're having a mixer … you know what that is?"

"Yeah, I know what that is."

"Okay. It's like a dance or a party. And some of the kids from other schools are coming, and I think I'd rather stay here this week-end if that's okay."

"I got it. You're still a little bit scared but not scared enough to come home and miss a party. How am I doing?"

"I knew you'd get it, Daddy. Would you settle it with Mamma? You always know what to say to her."

"Well, maybe not *always,* but in this case I can assure you it's in reliable hands."

"Thanks, Daddy. I gotta run. Gotta read thirty pages of English lit before three."

"You've got forty-five minutes, and you'll never do it. But I love you anyway. I'll call you tomorrow."

"Love you, Daddy. Bye."

As much as he wanted to see his daughter, J. D. felt something closer to relief than disappointment at her decision not to come home for the weekend. He knew Karlie would feel the same because they had so many other pressing things that needed to be dealt with. Certainly none of those things were more important than their only child's safety, but whatever this was brewing in his mind and threatening his reality, he knew that he couldn't ignore it and that Karlie *wouldn't* ignore it.

He needed to go back to the downtown restaurant and pick up Karlie. She had no other ride home if he didn't. But she would be all over him about the doctor's appointment she had probably already scheduled for him. He reached to his side and unclipped his cell phone, turned it off, and put it in the cup holder. With little recollection of driving there, he found himself turning onto Belmont Avenue. Did she say the last house on the left? And of all things, Belmont Avenue was a dead-end street.

→

He walked to the door of the brick two-story house with dormer windows and cracked walkway and banged the brass door knocker three times. Someone from inside yelled, "Coming!" just before the front door swung open to reveal a small gray-haired woman in shorts and a sweatshirt. She smiled up at him and took full control of the conversation with, "Good afternoon. Who are you, and how can I help you?"

"Are you Lavern Justice?"

"I am."

"I'm J. D. Wickman, and I've come to ask you about some property you used to own."

"Well, J. D. Wickman, you don't look like a serial killer, so would you like to come in?"

J. D. smiled and took her invitation as a compliment to his appearance and a credit to his general comportment and followed her to the living room just inside the door and to the left.

"Have a seat anyplace you like, J. D. Now what property are you interested in?"

"Out in the county about eighteen miles on Route 814. Your father used to own it, and then you owned it, and now there's a country store there."

"Okay." Lavern inserted this word in the conversation not so much as an approval of what had been said, but as a nod to continue.

"I'm interested in what was on that property before that store was there."

"Why?"

"I beg your pardon?" J. D. wasn't sure he had heard her correctly.

"Why? Why do you want to know what was there before?"

J. D. wasn't expecting this question and wasn't ready for it. He knew he couldn't tell her the truth because even he didn't know the truth. He looked this bright, friendly, no-frills lady in the eye and spoke.

"I think my grandmother used to live in a house out there, and I was just wondering if you might remember her."

"What's your grandmother's name?"

"She was Nettie Wickman."

"She could have. Lots of people lived out there before my time."

J. D. decided to get right to the point. "Wasn't there a house right near where Stan's shop is now?"

"I have no idea, young man. I haven't been out there for years."

"Well, there was a house out there when you sold it, wasn't there?"

"Can't be sure of that either. I was only ten years old when my father died and all that land was divided between my brothers and me. My name wound up on the deed, but it was all done by Daddy's law partners. I knew nothing about the sales or the property until I came of age and got the profits. I don't go out that way much anymore. Why are you researching where your grandmother lived?"

"It's just … ah, that, I'm doing a family tree. And just, you know, interested in my roots."

"Do you think there's some buried treasure out there, J. D.? Just what are your motives?"

"Motives? What do you mean?"

"What exactly are you looking for?"

J. D. was perspiring. This woman had an effect of authority on him—like an old schoolteacher or a strong mother figure. He wasn't comfortable lying to her and certainly wasn't comfortable confiding in her. But he had taken the deception too far to turn back. "I'm just researching all the different places she lived in the area. Putting a little booklet together for posterity."

Lavern Justice's eyes were stone, yet her smile was strangely warm. "Did your grandmother die there, Mr. Wickman?"

"Ah, no, I don't think so."

"You don't know where your grandmother died?"

"Ah, yes, I do, and no, it wasn't there."

"Mr. Wickman, I'm seventy-one years old. I've been around the block and down a few alleys, and I have a natural, built-in lie detector. And it's flashing red lights all over this room. You may not be a serial killer, but you're not on the level."

J. D. stood up and said, "Miss Justice, I thank you for your time. If I could tell you more, I would. And when I can, I will. For now, it's been a pleasure."

As J. D. turned around in her driveway, he could see her standing at the picture window watching him pull away. He didn't wave, but he did take note that the next time he turned into a street with a bright yellow rectangle sign that said "Dead End," he should pay closer attention.

Chapter Six

J. D. walked into the downtown Hanson Dining Club at five thirty and realized he had not eaten all day. Karlie had realized it too, because in the back booth where they both often sat and did daily receipts and read the local paper, she had a plate set for him. She was just placing his coffee on the table when he slid into the booth.

"Have you been to the doctor?"

"I could lie and tell you I have."

"No, you couldn't because I've already called his office and asked."

"So the question was just to see if I'd lie to you?"

"No, the question was to let you know just how worried I am

about you." She smiled, reached across the table, and rubbed his face. "I knew you wouldn't lie to me. How do you feel?"

"I never felt bad."

"J. D., now you *are* lying to me. You haven't been yourself for weeks. The headaches and those cold sweats in the middle of the night—and you don't even eat half the time anymore."

As if the issue had been settled and agreed upon, J. D. changed the subject abruptly to one he could be sure would trump the one at hand. "I talked to Angela this afternoon. She's not coming home this weekend."

Karlie dropped her hands to her lap, looked off at the wall, and sighed heavily. "I thought she was scared and just had to come home. Yesterday she even wanted to quit school for good."

"Well, that's old news. There's a party and she's a-stayin'." J. D. shrugged.

"Are you all right with that?" Karlie asked.

"You know, I am all right with it. I think she's dealt with it and she feels good about it all. She feels safe. And to be honest, honey, I don't need anything else to worry about right now."

"Well, let me give you one more thing or one less thing. Depends on how you look at it. I called Bobby Caywood, and he's coming down tonight to mark the bills, and then he'll be here in the morning with the three search warrants—and maybe by tomorrow at this time at least one of our problems will be over."

J. D. stopped eating and looked at his wife, torn between relief and anger. Relieved that she had finally seen it his way and angry because the last thing he told her this afternoon when she got out of the car was to do it *her* way.

"Honey, that's not what …"

"I know. That's not what you said to do earlier today, but I've been thinking, and I think you're right. This is how we should handle it. So there, I gave in to you on that one. Now will you give in to me on the next one?"

"Not if the next one is going to the doctor. You'll have to call in your debt on something else."

They ate in silence. A couple customers walked over to say hi, and one of the waitresses came by to ask a question, but there were no words spoken between them until they finished eating and J. D. broke the awkward silence.

"I rode around for an hour just before I came over here, and I've come up with an idea, something I have to try. But you have to listen to me and let me finish. I want you to let Bobby Caywood in tonight and mark the bills. I may or may not be here."

"Where are you going?"

"I said, let me finish. I'm going back out to the one lane bridge. I know you're thinking there *is* no one lane bridge. But I've got to be sure of something. Don't ask me to say too much because the more I say, the crazier I'm going to sound. Just trust me and let me have this freedom, and I'll tell you what I find when I get back tonight."

"J. D., if the house wasn't there this morning, why do you think it will be there tonight? Do you realize how insane this sounds?"

"No one realizes it more than me. But, Karlie, I think something tripped. I don't know what. But something tripped, and I think if I go out there at the very same time as I did last night and everything is the same, then maybe whatever tripped will trip again. I know that probably doesn't make sense. It barely makes sense to me. Just trust me when I tell you I'm all right, and I'll come home tonight and tell you everything I know."

Karlie Wickman sat for a long time, minutes maybe, and looked at her husband with what he recognized as love in her eyes. He sensed she wanted to give him words of encouragement and support, but none came. There was nothing she could say that would make a difference right now. So she nodded, smiled, got up, and cleared away the dishes.

$$\rightarrow$$

J. D. watched the odometer and the digital clock in the dashboard as he rounded the curves on the country road. One read seventeen miles; the other read 7:17 p.m. He couldn't be sure, but he strongly felt that the time of day had something to do with the mysterious appearance of the one lane bridge. It was twenty minutes after seven when he first came upon the bridge. The sun was in the exact same place, and now there was only one more mile to go until the road curved to the left. Around that bend he would come upon either a wide, two lane crossing with low concrete sides or a large, old-fashioned steel-trestle one lane bridge. He was prepared to be shocked either way.

And he was.

The one lane bridge towered before him as he stopped in the middle of the road. He was almost afraid to cross it. He was fearful it might not support him, that it might disappear just as he was in the middle of it. But he crept across at five miles per hour, watching the land and the stream on all sides. As he drove slowly down the small grade where the bridge ended and the county macadam resumed, he saw the dirt driveway to his right—the same driveway that this morning had been a paved parking lot in front of Stan's One Stop. His head hurt and his eyes were watering, but he made himself turn up the dusty little lane marked by weeds and vines on both sides. The muffler scraped on the loose dirt and gravel, but he hardly noticed. He was focused on the old frame house that was quickly coming into sight.

J. D. parked the van near an old tin cistern that looked like it was still in use. He sat for a moment before getting out, collecting his thoughts and preparing himself for whatever greeting, good or bad, he might face. As he closed the car door, the kitchen door opened, and Paul Clem stepped out on the porch. He looked shorter and thinner than he had yesterday and strangely older. The lines in his face were deeper and darker, and he was bareheaded. His hair was gray and thinning. When he spoke, his voice didn't have the friendly greeting it had yesterday when he had said, "Can I help you?" But J. D. had no reason to expect that same friendliness today. He had offended the man's sense of dignity and was now back standing in his yard, totally at his mercy.

"Mr. Clem. How are you doing, sir?"

"I'm fine. Do I know you?"

"Yes sir. My name is Wickman. John Wickman. I was here yesterday evening."

"You were? I don't remember you. You got the right house, young fellow?"

J. D. opened his mouth to offer a reply but suddenly realized he had none. He looked at all his surroundings to make sure he *was* at the right place because with all that had happened in the past twenty-four hours, he couldn't be certain. But of course he was. And this was the same man. Paul Clem. How else would J. D. have known his name?

"You *are* Paul Clem, aren't you?"

"That's right."

J. D. remembered the groceries in the back of the van and said, "I don't want you to take this wrong, but I have some food I brought that I want you to take."

"Are you from the church?"

"The church?"

"Yeah. The holy rollers down at New Park. They bring stuff up here all the time. If you are, thanks. And if you're not, thanks. I'll help you put 'em in the kitchen."

Paul ran his hand slowly over the fender of the van as J. D.'s breath quickened at what might be going through the old man's mind. They made the necessary repeat trips from the vehicle to the kitchen until all the groceries were stacked on the kitchen table.

J. D. saw a light shining through the beaded doorway that led into the parlor. He asked in a low voice as he set a final bag of canned goods on a kitchen chair, "How's your wife, Mr. Clem?"

Paul Clem looked at him with a quick jerk of his head. "What did you say, boy?"

"I said, how is your wife? Is she feeling any better or about the same?"

"Oh, she's feeling better, son. She's feeling a lot better. Ada's been dead for two years."

The stun from the words and the sting from Paul Clem's sarcastic attitude left J. D. dumbfounded. Was there some sort of misunderstanding? Was the woman from last night not his wife? Had he misconstrued who she was? No. He distinctly remembered him saying, "That's my wife. She's bedridden." What fresh hell was he going through now? He was about to turn and rush out the back door when someone called from the front parlor.

"Who is it, Daddy? Who's here?"

"Somebody from the church, honey. You go on back to sleep."

J. D. recognized the voice coming from the other room. And he knew he couldn't leave this house again with so many mysteries hanging thickly in the air. He looked at Paul with a sternness he had no right to express and said, "Who is that in there?"

"That's my daughter, if it's really any of your business."

"Your daughter, Lizzie?"

"The only one I got. Are you sure you're from the church?"

J. D. considered explaining everything he knew to this hardened man of the earth, but just as he was about to speak, the voice came from the other room.

"Daddy, send him in to see me."

J. D. stared into Paul's tired gray eyes. "Can I go see her?"

Paul began taking the food out of the plastic bags, pausing to examine the bags, and nodded his head without returning J. D.'s glare. J. D. wondered for just a moment if the plastic bags gave way to any suspicion in Paul Clem's mind. Certainly Paul had never seen anything like them before. Never had the question, paper or plastic? loomed so large in J. D.'s mind. He wished now he'd said "paper."

"Sure," Paul said. "It won't hurt nothing.'"

J. D. pushed back the strings of hanging beads and walked through the dark dining room, toward the single-bulb lamp in the far corner of the living room. The daybed was in the same position by the front door, but a different person was lying in it. This time it was Lizzie, and she looked different. Prettier. Longer hair. Fuller cheeks.

"Lizzie?"

She smiled and sat up. "Hi. I know you. Your name starts with a W."

"That's right. Wickman. John Wickman."

"I remember you real well. You had that funny-lookin' car."

"Lizzie, where's your mother?"

"Mamma died nearly two years ago. Did you know my mamma?"

"Well, I met her once. She was right here in that very same bed when I was here yesterday."

"Yesterday? Do you mean that in a poetic way, Mr. Wickman? My schoolteacher talks like that sometimes when he's readin' poetry and stuff. He says 'yesterday' when he means 'a long time ago.' Is that what you were doin'?"

J. D. heard the back door close. He looked at her more intently than he ever had before and tried to find reason and good sense in the conversation they were having.

"Lizzie, listen to me. How long has it been since you saw me last? How long since I was out here in your kitchen and you were frying bread?"

"Is that what I was frying when you were here? I didn't remember that, but I love fried bread."

"Lizzie, listen to me. How long ago was that?"

"Oh, it must have been two years ago anyway, if Mamma was still alive."

"It wasn't just yesterday?" J. D. was beginning to feel frantic but hoped his voice didn't show it.

"Why, of course not. Yesterday I was here in bed. Mamma died when I was fourteen. That was two years ago."

J. D. took a deep breath and asked the question he knew he had to ask but was in mortal fear of hearing the answer.

"Lizzie, what year did your mamma die?"

"The fall of 1940."

Something grabbed J. D. in the hollow of his stomach, and he thought he might be sick. He felt a shiver from deep in his spine, and he knew his voice was shaky when he took a deep breath and asked, "So what is today's date?"

"You mean you don't know what today is? Today is Thursday."

"No. I mean the *date*. Do you have a calendar?"

"There's a calendar on the back of the door. The one with the pretty pictures. It's September tenth, 1942."

Where was he? How did he get here? What was that bridge? A doorway? A portal through time? And why? Why was he here, and who were these people?

"Lizzie, do you remember me being here before?"

"I said I did."

"But your father doesn't."

"Well, that was a couple years ago, and Daddy's failed a lot since Mamma passed. Plus he don't like a lot of people. He's kind of gruff."

He looked at this pretty young girl lying in a sickbed yet still full of conversation and personality. "Why are you in bed here in the parlor?"

"I hurt my foot about a week ago. I was working up in the barn and stepped on a nail. It was rusty, and boy, was it big. It went clear through my foot. Wanna see? It went in the bottom and came out the top. Daddy pulled it out."

She drew the sheets back to reveal a swollen foot bandaged with gauze and wrapping. There were bloodstains on the top and bottom. He could tell she was in pain as she grimaced while trying to lift her foot to show him.

"Has a doctor seen you?"

"Doctors cost a lot of money, and I don't know what they can do for me."

Those were almost the exact words Paul had answered with when J. D. had asked if a doctor had seen Ada. J. D. had left then without taking any action, and some time had passed—just a day to him, but two years to the Clems! And now, Ada was dead. Lizzie needed a doctor, and soon. He couldn't leave her here like he had her mother.

"Where did your father go, Lizzie?"

"Out back, milking probably. You'll see him out there some-where. Are you leaving now?"

"Maybe. I need to talk with him, but I'll see you before I go."

"Thanks for the food. Tell all of them at the church I said, 'bless 'em.'"

J. D. walked into the kitchen. As he neared the door leading to the back porch, he heard something he faintly remembered from yesterday. A radio. It was turned down low, and he had to stop to hear what was on. It was Ernest Tubb singing, "Walking The Floor Over You." What he had assumed to be a traditional country music station yesterday—a "classic" country station—was actually a regular country music station playing current hits. *Hits from 1942!* His knees nearly buckled.

He found Paul carrying a bucket of chicken feed out of a shed in the backyard. The look on his face was just as fierce and unfriendly as it had been when he met J. D. at the van. Life had whipped him and left him blowing in the wind. He had lost his wife, and now his daughter was flat on her back, fighting what could be a losing battle. The look in his cold, empty eyes said he had no reason to get out of bed each morning, yet he walked through his duties as man of the house. J. D. spoke to him with apprehension. He wasn't expecting a positive answer, but he did hope the negative would not be violent.

"Mr. Clem. Lizzie is a very sick girl. She may have blood poisoning. She needs to see a doctor. Can I take her to see one?"

"Take her? No. You're not taking her anywhere. You think I'm turnin' my daughter loose with some stranger and lettin' her get in that station wagon or whatever that is with you?"

"You can come along. We'll just be gone for a little while. Just long enough to get her to the emergency room."

J. D.'s back stiffened at what he had just proposed. What if the old man took him up on his offer and all three of them went into town? How could he explain what was happening and all the sights he would see? The highways, the cars, the houses, the buildings? How could he explain something he didn't understand himself?

"She'll be fine. I'll take care of her. Always have."

"I know you have, sir. But she needs something you can't give her this time. She needs a doctor as soon as possible. If you won't let me take her to see one, then let me bring one out here."

"Doctors cost money."

"I'll pay."

"I think you need to go."

"I'm not leaving here without her."

Paul Clem set the small pail on the ground by his feet, stood with his shoulders squared, and raised his height a good two inches. His eyes narrowed and there was flint in his voice. "You got any kids?"

"Yes, I do. I have a daughter not much older than Lizzie."

"Then you'll understand what I'm about to tell you. You try to move my girl from that room, and you gotta kill me to do it."

J. D. knew he meant it. He would have to bring the doctor to Lizzie. He only hoped he had time. If one day on his side of the bridge was two years on hers, he didn't. But maybe it wasn't quite so simple an equation. In the past twenty-four hours, nothing had been. He would have to try. Maybe he had time. Maybe he did.

Chapter Seven

J. D. recalled nothing of the thirty-minute drive back to Hanson. One second he was crossing the one lane bridge, and the next he was pulling into the parking lot behind the Dining Club. His eyes had apparently been on the road, but his mind was on Lizzie and how to explain it all to Karlie. He knew there was a young girl across that bridge who desperately needed medical attention, but he had no way of proving that to his skeptical wife. He had promised to tell her all about it when he got back, but what would he say? He felt like the little boy in a joke he had heard. When the boy's mother asked him what he had learned in Sunday school, he said they had talked about Moses and how when he got to the Red Sea he had his army build a pontoon bridge and carry all the people across the water.

Then he had his army blow up the bridge so the bad guys couldn't cross. His mother said, "Are you sure that's what they taught you this morning?" And the little boy said, "No, but if I told you what really happened, you'd never believe it."

He sat in the car and wished he still smoked.

$$\rightarrow$$

The last employee exited through the back door just minutes before Officer Bobby Caywood pulled up alongside J. D.'s van. They got out of their vehicles and walked into the restaurant together. J. D. was thankful for the company as it gave him a few more minutes before he had to talk to Karlie alone.

"Hey, honey, Bobby's here," J. D. called as he locked the door behind him.

Karlie came out of the kitchen and said, "Hi, Bobby. Are you ready to do this?"

She didn't look at J. D. He knew her well enough to know that while he was gone, her thoughts had congealed to a cold silence— and he was in for a rough night. And his mind was more on how much of the truth he could tell Karlie than on the money they were here to protect. The whole truth just might prompt her to commit him before morning. And he wasn't even sure what a half-truth would be at this point. But he had to push those thoughts away. They were here to mark bills and catch an embezzler, a disloyal employee. They were here to bring the hatchet down while Lizzie Clem lay dying somewhere in the 1940s. What was he thinking? He couldn't possibly tell Karlie that. A girl died sixty-five years ago, but she was still alive tonight? Maybe he *did* need to be committed. And what had Caywood just said to him?

"Did you hear me, J. D.?"

"No, I'm sorry, Bobby, I didn't."

"I said, would you put a mark on these bills? I'm going to mark them, and I want you to also. Keeping it all on the up and up so there's no chance for a mistake."

"Sure. Karlie, do you want to mark them?"

Karlie was nowhere to be seen. She had gone back into the kitchen to turn out lights and close pantry doors. She was keeping her distance. When J. D.'s mind returned again to the business at hand, Officer Caywood was talking again.

"… does their shift end?"

"What's that?"

"The girls that open up in the morning. What time does their shift end?"

"One o'clock."

"Okay, why don't I meet you over here at five minutes to one tomorrow afternoon? We'll stop them as they leave the building and take them into the office and make our move. That way the evening shift will be here on the floor, and whatever happens doesn't disturb business."

"Sounds good to me." J. D. raised his voice a little and said, "Sound all right to you, honey?" But "honey" wasn't responding. The only answer he got was another pantry door slamming somewhere in the back and another light being switched off.

$\rightarrow$

J. D. drove Karlie to the Kroger parking lot to pick up the BMW they had left there that morning. Words were not exchanged, but the feelings were heavy in the air. Karlie opened the car door and was about to get out when she finally found her voice.

"J. D., are we going to go home and go to bed and never talk more about where you were all evening? Because if we are, I don't think I can take it."

"I don't know where I was."

This elicited no response—only a stony stare and silence.

J. D. continued, "I went out there and, honey, you have to believe me. The bridge was there. The one lane bridge. I drove over it, and the house was there. And the man was there and the daughter. But the woman … the woman was dead. I talked to the girl. She's sixteen now, and she's in bed like her mother was before, and the man looks old and tired. And … and it's two years later. They're both two years older, but only a day has passed."

J. D. could only see shadows on his wife's face, but he didn't have to see her clearly to know what was in her mind. The sobs that began to rock her body told him all he needed to know. He couldn't blame her. He reached for her, but she didn't move toward him. She just kept crying until he suddenly realized he was crying too. Tears he hadn't felt since his father's funeral eight years ago were running down his cheeks and falling on his hands. His wife was sick with concern, he was confused and scared, and their marriage was in danger of crumbling around him as surely as was everything he had come to know as normal. His mind was full of questions and empty of answers. But he couldn't ignore what he had seen with his own eyes. His wife needed the man she had two days ago, but a young girl somewhere out on Route 814 in 1942 needed a doctor, and he was the only person on earth who could help her. If indeed this was still earth.

Chapter Eight

J. D. wasn't sure either one of them slept that night. He knew for certain they didn't talk, and he was almost certain neither of them drifted off. Even a restless sleep—the kind that lasted for only minutes before he found himself looking at the alarm clock for the twentieth time that night—would have been welcome. But he heard every automobile that passed, every boom of a teenager's heavy-duty car radio that jarred the walls of the house, and every door shutting at the neighbor's from dawn on. At six thirty he climbed out of bed as quietly as he could, showered, dressed, and went to the kitchen to watch TV and drink instant coffee just to kill time until he was sure his old friend Jack Hamish was out of bed and at the drugstore.

At eight forty-five he walked into Alden Drugs and waited till Jack was off the phone. When Jack looked up and saw J. D., he motioned for him to come behind the counter and up the steps to his office. J. D. smiled and followed the instructions, sitting down in front of the big, old wooden desk full of files and papers. He looked at the framed diplomas and licenses on the wall and the framed pictures of Jack's two nephews on the desk.

He and Jack shared a long history. They had sat directly across the aisle from each other in the first grade, and Jack enjoyed, almost from day one, kicking J. D.'s books out from under his desk every time he passed. After the fourth time, J. D. returned the kick and sent Jack's books flying across the aisle just as the teacher looked up. J. D. was caught and punished, and that day at lunch Jack had come up to him and apologized for causing trouble. Their friendship began in that moment and lasted through grade school, high school, and college.

They still ate lunch together a couple of times a week and played poker together every first Friday of the month. Jack Hamish was his closest friend, the one he would confide this baffling situation to even if Jack couldn't help him. Or maybe he could. Jack was a pharmacist and exactly what J. D. needed at this very moment. But he dreaded trying to explain *why* he needed him.

"Hey, buddy, how you doing? Sorry to keep you waiting. Want some coffee?"

"No. I've had plenty."

"You look like you've been up all night."

J. D. gave him a half smile and admitted he had. Then, to answer Jack's question of why, he began to tell his story as honestly and as convincingly as possible.

"I was out riding in the country a couple of days ago and broke down out on Route 814. You know where that is?"

"Maybe. Is it out there where …?"

"It doesn't really matter," J. D. interrupted. "It's about eighteen miles northeast. Anyway, I was driving the Triumph, and I broke down and didn't have a signal on my cell. So I went up to a house and an old farmer met me in the yard."

Jack's grin went as wide as his face. "Is this going to be a farmer's daughter joke?"

J. D. cut him off. "No. I wish it were. He had a daughter, but she was like fourteen years old. And he had a wife who was sick in bed, and they were as poor as dirt and needy as any family you've ever seen. Like those families our Sunday school class used to shop for at Christmas when we were kids. They needed food, but the old man was proud and kind of ran me off when I offered to help. So I came home and told Karlie about them, and we bought them some groceries and went out there yesterday morning. And here's where it gets strange. They were gone. They weren't there any longer."

"They had moved?" Jack asked with a slight shrug.

J. D. looked at his old friend a long time before he answered. So long that Jack became uneasy. "So what is it? Had they moved or not?"

J. D. rubbed his face, feeling the sleepless hours that lay behind him. He chose his words as if he were a lawyer defending the case of his life.

"They had disappeared. They were gone. Their house was gone. A store was where their house was. And even this enormous old one

lane steel bridge you had to cross to get to them was gone. Just …
gone."

Jack's wide smile was gone too. His lips were tight, and his
eyes were slits as if he was trying to see into his friend's mind. J. D.
watched every twitch in the face of the friend sitting across the desk
from him. He was imagining every thought that was going through
his old buddy's brain. He knew Jack would try not to be critical or
judgmental, and at one point he even expected a punch line from his
lips to ease the tension. But that didn't come. After a long couple of
seconds past comfortable, Jack said, "I don't get it."

"Neither do I, buddy," J. D. said with a heaviness he was sure
even Jack had never heard before.

Jack looked down at his desk as if the answer was somewhere in
its disarray and then slowly brought his eyes up to meet his friend's.
He spoke in a tone and a manner usually reserved for trying to make
a point with a child.

"You found a farmhouse and a family one day, and the next they
were all gone. What exactly are you trying to tell me?"

"What I'm *really* trying to tell you is what I haven't actually told
you yet. If you think I'm ready for the nut bin now, wait till you hear
the rest of it. I went back again. That time I was able to cross over
and this teenage girl—her name is Lizzie—told me what year it was
while I was out there. It was 1940 the first time I went and 1942 the
second time. And then when I cross back over that bridge, heading
home, it's *now* again."

Jack stared straight into his eyes and said, "Hey, you're Michael
J. McFly. and you just cracked the time barrier. Is that what you're
telling me?"

"Yeah, something like that—except I'm not kidding. I'm dead serious. I was there, and I talked to these people, and I went back the second time and saw them again. Jack, you know how we've talked so many times about how we'd like to go back in time, and if we could where we'd like to go to and what we'd like to see?"

Jack leaned back in his worn, high-back desk chair and crossed his hands in his lap. "Yes, my friend, but we were playing a game of what-if."

They heard a bell ring, and Jack stood up. "I've got a customer. Wait here."

J. D. sat in misery while his friend took Mrs. Marguerite Troller's empty bottle of Atenolol and told her it would be ready in thirty minutes. Then just as he was about to come back up the steps, someone else came in looking for Zeasorb powder and an ear syringe. All of this took only four minutes, but to J. D. it seemed an hour. When Jack was finished, he came back to the office, closed the door, and said in a low voice, "Okay, so what if I believe you? What do we do?"

Not "what do you want me to do" or "what are you going to do," but "what do *we* do." Jack Hamish was a true friend.

"I know how crazy all this sounds, Jack, and I appreciate you listening. Here's the deal. The girl is sick. She ran a nail through her foot. All the way through it. And there're lines already starting up her leg. And that's bad, isn't it?"

Jack was as serious now as his friend across the desk. "Could be septicemia."

"What's that?"

"Blood poisoning."

"One day on this side of the bridge equaled two years on the other side. If that holds, the girl will be dead before we can get to her. I just have to hope and pray that part of it doesn't hold. Her daddy wouldn't let me bring her with me to see a doctor, but he can't refuse medicine if I take it out there and give it to her. Well, I suppose he could. He could fight me giving it to her, but I would have to find a way to do it anyway and worry about the consequences later." J. D. paused and looked at his friend. "What medicine do I take her?"

Jack rubbed his head with both hands and said, "Some form of PCN."

"What's that?"

"I'm sorry. Penicillin."

"Talk to me in simple terms."

"Well, there're all kinds of penicillin. You could find a doctor and ask him for a prescription for, I don't know, benzylpenicillin for instance. He could give her a heavy dose of that, and that should take care of her."

J. D. looked at his old friend long and hard. The silence across the desk was finally broken when the pharmacist said, "What? What else do you want me to do?"

"Get a doctor?" J. D. asked sarcastically. "Go back over the bridge and find a doctor in 1942, and get him to give me a prescription, and then go somewhere and get it filled? Is that what you're saying I need to do?"

Jack was waving his hand in the air. "Wait. Go back. Did you say 1942?"

"Yeah," J. D. said, more as an angry commentary on Jack's attitude than as an answer.

"There was no penicillin in 1942. Not for the public, anyway. It had just been discovered and introduced to the U.S., but it was all being used on the soldiers. The public saw hardly any of it till after the war. This girl is not apt to get a prescription as there probably is none to be had on the home front, if you follow what I'm saying."

"Jack, if you follow what *I'm* saying, none of that matters. I'm not going to look for a doctor back there. I'm going to take the medicine with me in my pocket. All I need is for you to go over to one of these shelves and give me a bottle of whatever you think will work, and we're in business."

"Whoa, whoa, whoa, whoa. Not gonna happen, amigo. I don't give drugs to friends, and you know that. Never have. Never will."

"And I've never asked you for any. But you have to admit this is kind of a special situation."

"'Special situation' is an understatement, old friend. It's a crazy situation and a crazy request. And if anyone else came to me with this story, I'd report them and have them locked up before lunchtime."

"So you think I'm crazy too?"

"Of course I think you're crazy, and apparently someone else does also or you wouldn't have said 'too.'"

"Karlie."

"Good woman."

And then everything came to a standstill. The little office above Alden's Drugs was silent, and the two friends, who had never run out of something to talk about in forty years, were suddenly mute. Neither moved, and neither blinked. J. D. was the one with the most to lose, so he spoke first.

"Will you help me?"

"Do what?"

"Will you give me a bottle of penicillin?"

"No. But I'll go out there with you and take a bottle."

"Thank you, buddy. You don't know what this means to me."

Jack shook his head and smiled. "You want to go right after lunch?"

It was J. D.'s turn to shake his head. "No. We can't go until after supper. We need to arrive at the bridge at exactly twenty minutes after seven. I think that's why Karlie and I couldn't find it. I think it has to be a certain time of the day."

"You really are crazy, aren't you, J. D.?"

J. D. stood up to leave, and they shook hands. Something they seldom did. As he went out the door of the office, he said over his shoulder, "You're the Jonathan to my David. I owe you one."

"Big time," Jack assured him.

"I'll pick you up at six forty-five."

Chapter Nine

Katherine Kimball was the first employee J. D. and Karlie had hired over five years before when they opened the Dining Club Restaurant on the west end of Hanson. She was there when the original kitchen equipment was installed and had worked late nights with the two of them, setting up the tables and booths, hanging the light fixtures, and finding the old train photos that decorated the walls. She had cooked when the kitchen help was sick, waited tables when waitresses quit without warning, and all the time kept up the duties of hostess on any shift where she was needed. Two years ago when they found the spot on Main for their second location, she had managed the west end alone while Karlie and J. D. set up the new restaurant. Then she had come to the downtown Dining Club as the morning hostess and had given them the time they needed to see to both branches of their dream. Katherine was fifty years old and had been a single mother since her twin sons were ten years of age. Her husband had left her one night without even a note of explanation while she was working as a waitress at one of the oldest dining rooms in town. Restaurants had been her life, and that was why the Wickmans sought her out when they decided to go into business for themselves. She had been their pillar, and they had known her and her family most of their lives. If Katherine were the one stealing money from the cashbox, it would break their hearts on more than one level. Still, they had no choice but to treat her the same as the other two in the present situation.

Lottie Arello was not a classmate of either Karlie or J. D., but they had known her since high school. She was a few years behind them and had moved away from Hanson right after graduation. She lived and worked in Charlotte for a while, where she met her husband, and they had moved back to the area four years ago to be close to her aging parents. Randy, her husband, had taken on two jobs to make up for the income they lost by relocating to a smaller town, and eventually Lottie realized she, too, would have to get a job. She had run into Karlie at the morning YMCA aerobics class they both attended and asked if there was any chance of getting hired on at the restaurant. At the time there were no openings, but Karlie told her she would keep her in mind. When the Main Street Dining Club was about to open, Karlie remembered and hired her without asking for references. She had always been a good worker and was never late and never short with customers. In fact, many of the regulars bragged on what a nice and personable person she was and always asked to be seated in her area. If Lottie was their culprit, J. D. knew Karlie would take it even harder than if it was Katherine.

Crystal Gleason had only been there nine months. She was nine-teen years old. Pretty. Slim. Short blonde hair. Glasses. And teeth that smiled even when she didn't. She charmed just by walking up to the table. Every young boy and old man wanted Crystal to wait on them. They joked with her, and she gave it back with good humor and an easy laugh. Truth be known, she was the highest-tipped wait-ress they had at either location. She was attentive to a fault and kept her tables and the floor area spotless, even after a table with tots had trashed the chairs and the hardwood oak underfoot. Crystal dated no one in particular but always preferred the morning shift so she could have her evenings free for whatever nightlife she enjoyed. They rarely saw her out except at an occasional movie with a group of friends. College was not in her future, but it was easy to see that marriage to whomever she might choose was. She exuded personality and sweet-ness. If her hands were in the till, she was going to disappoint a lot of people, young and old.

J. D. and Karlie sat in their back booth saying little to each other. The giant railroad-watch clock on the wall over the front door said it was 12:40 p.m. The uneasy silence between them made J. D. wonder if Karlie was having the same thoughts he was having ... but neither of them was expressing them out loud. Their silence was broken at twelve forty-five when Bobby Caywood came in the front door and took a seat in the first booth on the right. Seconds later, J. D.'s cell phone rang.

"How do you want to do this? I have the warrants in my pocket. I can stop them as they're going out the front or back door and take them in your office, or you and Karlie can do it. Or we can all three do it together. It's your call."

"Karlie and I will take care of it."

"Okay. I'll stay here, and if anyone refuses to let you look in their purse or search their person, you just open the office door and I'll come back with the warrants."

"I hope we won't need to do it that way."

"Me, too. But don't be surprised at whatever happens. You trap something, and it's bound to fight back. There may be a scene. So be ready for that."

"I know. I'll go tell them that we want to see them before they leave."

"No. Don't do it yet. Wait till the last minute. Wait till they're ready to go out the door. You don't want to give anybody the chance to ditch the evidence. You've got to find it on them. Understand?"

"Yes."

"Ask Karlie if she understands, and tell her to nod to me. It's important we're all on the same page here."

J. D. hung up the phone, leaned into the table, and related all this to his wife. She looked across the restaurant at Caywood and nodded her approval without a smile or any show of emotion. The chase was on.

→

Katherine stopped at their booth to say good-bye.

"You kids look a little haggard today. Up all night sparrin' or sparkin'?"

"A little of both," J. D. managed. Karlie hung her head and said nothing. He knew she wasn't going to be able to pull this off. Her heart was not in it. She loved Katherine like a favorite aunt. Maybe her way was best, after all. Just tell them outright what was going on and make it stop instead of trying to find out who the thief was. But it was too late now.

"Katherine." J. D. struggled with his breathing. Confronting someone with bad news was always harder than he thought it would be. Especially when it was someone he liked and respected. "Katherine, we need to see you in the office before you leave." He got up and walked to the office door in the back.

Katherine looked at Karlie, who was sliding out of the booth with her eyes averted. She looked from one to the other and said, "Sure," and walked in front of Karlie, past J. D., who was holding the door.

He looked toward the kitchen and saw Crystal gathering her sweater and purse from behind the counter. He figured Lottie must be somewhere in the kitchen.

"Crystal. We need to see you in the office before you leave."

She looked up and, with the same pleasant smile she always carried, said, "All right."

Just then Lottie came out of the kitchen with her handbag and a Styrofoam sandwich container in her hand.

"Lottie, can I see you in the office for a minute?"

Without a word of consent she walked past him and through the door but stopped when she saw the other three women already standing inside. She turned and said to J. D., "What's going on?"

"We need to talk to you. Come on in so I can close the door."

She did, and they all three stood with Karlie and looked to J. D. for some sort of instruction or explanation.

"Sit down. All of you. Find a chair someplace."

Katherine was the first to speak. "What's up, J. D.?"

"This is not easy for me. For us. But it has to be done. We have a little problem. And we have narrowed it down to the morning shift. I don't know how to say it except to just say it. We have money missing and a lot of it."

Two of the women gasped, and for the life of him he couldn't tell which two. He was pretty sure it was Crystal and Lottie. But did it matter? Surprise could make them gasp, and by this time the guilty party would know what was happening and could have faked a gasp. He was about to continue when Karlie spoke up from where she was standing behind them.

"Katherine, Lottie, Crystal, we have been watching this for some time now, and we know that someone, and we're pretty sure it's someone in this room, has been taking money from the cash box in the mornings. The last thing in the world we want is to hurt anyone's feelings. And as sure as someone is guilty, we know that probably two are innocent, and we realize what a chance we're taking here … but we know no better way to do this."

The last five words of her sentence were barely audible. Tears were standing in Karlie's eyes, and her voice was shaking. She was doing what she had promised to do with as much conviction as she could muster. J. D. was proud of her and felt a need to rescue her.

"What Karlie is saying is we are doing what we *have* to do. It makes us both sick to have to do it, but we didn't ask for any of this to happen. I wish we had another room where we could go and do this privately, but we don't. So I am going to ask each of you to open your purses and let us look through them and your pockets."

Lottie spoke up. "And if we refuse to let you search us like common criminals?"

"Then we'll do it legal. We have a police officer on the premises with warrants. We don't want to do that unless we have to. Unless you force us to." J. D. was as firm and friendly as he could be with the little bit of anger that was seeping into his voice at Lottie's challenge. He looked at each of the ladies in question and said, "Who wants to go first?"

Nobody moved. Nobody volunteered. Crystal looked at Katherine for guidance. Katherine turned and looked at Karlie, and Lottie continued to glare at J. D.

"J. D., I can't believe you're doing this," Katherine said as she opened her purse and dumped the contents onto the desktop. Lipstick, compact, notepads, ballpoint pens, loose change, and a billfold hit the ink blotter and scattered.

"Open up the billfold and take the bills out, Katherine." J. D. waited for her to do as she was asked, but she didn't budge.

"You've gone this far. You take it out yourself." She was defiant and angry.

"Katherine, I'm not going into your billfold. If you insist on doing it this way, we'll bring the police into it. I'll have Caywood step in here and make it official."

Karlie spoke through her tears and pleaded, "Please, Katherine. Just do it yourself, and don't make this any harder on any of us."

Without looking up, Katherine Kimball reached down, took the money from her billfold, and placed the bills one by one the desk as if she were counting money back to a customer. Four twenties, one five, and four ones. Eighty-nine dollars.

"Do you want to see the change?" she asked with a sarcastic tone.

"No," J. D. assured her. "Put it back in your purse."

"Wait. Don't you want to frisk me?"

"Katherine, please," Karlie pleaded again.

"Crystal. Lottie. One of you go next," J. D. demanded more than asked.

Crystal stepped toward the desk and dumped her oversized Gucci rip-off on the same spot where Katherine had just retrieved her belongings. The contents were similar to Katherine's, plus a packet of tissues and car keys and loose bills on top of the pile. The loose bills had been in the bottom of the purse.

"Why do you have loose money in your purse like that, Crystal?"

"Tips. I keep my purse behind the counter and just stick my tips in there 'cause I don't have any pockets."

"Count it out like Katherine did."

She began turning over each bill, fives and ones galore. There on six twenties and three ten-dollar bills were the little circles and the little crosses that J. D. and Bobby had etched with a Magic Marker just sixteen hours before. Only J. D. and Karlie knew the significance of those tiny marks. They glanced at each other, but neither said a word. J. D.'s first instinct was to call off the search. The thief had been found. But then better sense prevailed, and he realized it was entirely possible that two people *could* be guilty. So he simply told Crystal to gather her things and then turned to Lottie, who followed suit without a word. Her purse was sparse, carrying no makeup and no pens. She had keys and a small change purse that housed her driver's license and three folded tens, six fives, and ten one-dollar bills. She spread them out one by one and then stood looking off into space until J. D. told her to put everything back in her bag.

"What now? Do we all go to jail?" Katherine asked with a sneer.

"No. You can go home, Katherine," J. D. answered just as curtly.

"And I may stay home."

"That's your choice. We told you this was not easy for us before we even started." J. D.'s words were coming faster, and his voice was rising with each syllable. "We didn't ask for this problem, and we didn't know any better way of doing it. If you were in our position, you would have done the same thing."

"Yeah, I might have done the same thing, but I don't think I'd have done it the same way. This is pretty insulting, J. D."

"So is getting robbed, Katherine. So if you want to quit, if you want to stay home, you go right ahead. No one has done anything to you. And frankly, I'm just a little bit tired of your attitude."

Katherine turned on her heel and walked out of the office door. Lottie looked at J. D. and then at Karlie and, without saying anything to anyone, turned and did the same. It was only Crystal who asked, "Can we *all* go?"

"No, Crystal. Sit down. And lay your money out on the table again."

What Bobby Caywood saw from his vantage point in the first booth to the right of the front door was a tight-faced Katherine Kimball storming the length of the restaurant and exiting the main door without turning her head in either direction. Lottie Arello took a short right turn and exited the back door leading to the parking lot.

The office door closed again. It was maybe thirty seconds before he was jolted from his sitting position along with a dozen other customers by a spine-cringing scream from behind the office door.

He ran toward it.

Chapter Ten

Crystal was standing in the middle of the floor with her fists by the sides of her head screaming, "No! No! No!" when Bobby Caywood burst through the doorway. Karlie was reaching for her and trying to calm her hysteria by putting her arms around her. J. D. was standing helplessly, watching the uncontrollable situation unfold.

"Crystal, calm down now. Just calm down." Crystal fell rather than sat in the chair behind her and buried her head in her hands and resorted to quiet sobs. J. D. handed her some tissues, and Caywood leaned against the door.

Crystal looked up with red eyes and scanned each face in the room. Finally she said, "I did not take that money. I've never stolen anything in my life."

"Then how do you explain it being in your purse, Crystal?" J. D. asked with just a tinge of impatience.

"I don't know. Somebody put it in there."

"Who would put money in your purse?"

"Whoever stole it."

"Crystal, does that make any sense to you? Somebody steals money and puts it in *your* purse instead of their own? How stupid do you think we are?" asked J. D.

"I don't know. I mean, I don't think you're stupid, but I think somebody is smarter than you think they are."

"What do you mean by that, honey?" Karlie asked as she walked behind the girl and rubbed her shoulders like a mother consoling a child.

"I mean I know I didn't take that money. Whoever took it stuffed it in my bag when I wasn't looking."

Detective Caywood spoke next. "Have you found money in your purse that wasn't yours before?"

"No."

"Then why today?"

"I don't know."

"Crystal," J. D. said as he sat down in a chair in front of her, "you have to know what this looks like to us. What would you do if you were us? Would you believe what you're saying right now?"

"I guess not." Crystal showed signs of calming as the sobs abated. "But somebody must have gotten scared and thought you all were getting close to them, and they got rid of the money so you wouldn't find it on them."

"When would anyone have had a chance to do that?"

"Maybe when they saw Mr. Caywood come in and sit down just before shift change."

"Mr. Caywood comes in often, Crystal," Karlie said. "Why would anyone think anything was odd about that?

"Well, he didn't sit at the counter the way he usually does, but I just thought he was waiting on someone else to join him. But if I had been guilty of something, I might have thought something was up. You know what I mean?"

J. D. turned and looked up at Caywood and said with a mixture of sarcasm and tension-breaking humor, "Good job, Caywood. You want to take it from here?"

Bobby crossed his arms and didn't respond to J. D.'s remark but took it as an opening to address Crystal again.

"Everybody who breaks the law always claims they're innocent. Circumstantial. Red-handed. Whatever the evidence may be, they always tell you somebody else is to blame and that they're victims. Crystal, you're not a criminal at heart. You're a sweet girl who has done an irresponsible thing. So be honest with these folks. I think I know them well enough to assure you it can be solved right here in this room. Just be honest."

Crystal looked up with tears streaming down her young, pretty face and dripping off her chin. She looked directly into J. D.'s eyes and said, "Mr. Wickman, you don't have any idea what it's like to be telling someone the truth with all your heart and they just won't believe you. I don't know what else I can say to make you not doubt me. No matter how unbelievable it all sounds and looks, as sure as there's a God in heaven, I didn't take that money."

A strange stillness came over the room. J. D. Wickman, copro-prietor and recent bearer of his own hard-to-believe story, looked at his wife, who was staring at him through tears. No one spoke, but even if they had, J. D. would not have heard anything but a replay of Crystal's plea. His ears were full of her words, and his heart was full of her feelings. He truly believed this girl was innocent. And if she wasn't? Chances were she was scared enough right now that she would never do anything like this again. But wasn't this exactly what Karlie had been saying from the beginning? Wasn't it her notion from the start that just the fear of getting caught would stop the stealing, and a good person who had done "an irresponsible thing," as Caywood had put it, would see the light and all would be well? Was it possible that he was wrong for bringing this unfortunate situation this far? Or was he changing his mind just because he could relate to the frustration Crystal was feeling in not being able to find anyone who would believe her story?

"Crystal, I want you to go wash your face and then go home," said J. D. "And then I want you back here at six in the morning ready to go to work."

She looked at him with a childish innocence that made him feel worse than he'd felt since the whole thing had begun and said, "Do you mean it?"

"Yes, I mean it. It's over. We'll see you tomorrow."

Crystal gathered her belongings and went out the office door, closing it softly behind her. Bobby Caywood moved just enough to let her squeeze by. He was the first to speak after she left the room.

"You know what this means, don't you? You still have money missing, and you don't know who took it."

"I know Crystal didn't," said J. D.

"Do you?"

"No, not really," J. D. admitted.

"And if she didn't, one of the other two did. Either way you've got a thief working for you and handling your money."

"And so did Jesus. So what?" J. D. was frustrated and defiant and realized he was striking out at the very person who was trying to help him.

"I could say 'and look where that got *Him,*' but I won't." Bobby was protecting his territory, but his calm expression told J. D. he knew this was a difficult situation for them. Bobby would support whatever they decided.

"Do you want me to talk to the other two women?"

"No. Thank you, Bobby, for being here, but as far as we're concerned, it's over. We're going to let it go." He looked to Karlie for her nod of consent and got it, plus a smile.

"They may not come back, you know," Caywood warned. "You may never see the three of them again. Just because *you* think it's over, they may not think so."

"Well, if that's the case, then we might need you to wait tables till we can find some more help."

They laughed nervously at this and welcomed the much-needed tension breaker. Bobby Caywood said, as he was opening the door to leave, "And, hey, I'm sorry about that sitting-at-the-counter thing. That girl was smarter than I thought she was."

"Yeah, she just might be smarter than we all thought she was."

And then there were two. Karlie came over to J. D. and put her arms around him and said, "I love you more right this minute than I did even the day our daughter was born."

He held her. "I might have done the dumbest thing I've ever done in my life here today."

"I don't care. I love you for it even if it was wrong."

"Thank you. I love you, too.

"Can I ask you something?"

"Sure. Anything."

"When you went out to that … house … out in the country last night … the van was full of groceries. Those groceries were gone this morning." She paused. "Where are those groceries?"

J. D. waited a long time before he answered. He weighed the question and decided against three or four possible responses, all the time never letting her go from their embrace. "You may *love* me more right now than you ever have, but you don't believe me any more than you ever did."

"I want to."

"I know you do, honey. I know you do."

Chapter Eleven

Angela Wickman sat in the passenger seat with her purse and a small suitcase crowding her feet. She watched the houses, pastures, billboards, and utility poles whiz by the side window as the radio blasted song after song toward her inattentive ear. She could never remember feeling lonelier. She had always wished she had an older sister. Even pretended that she did. She would talk to her the same way kids often talked to imaginary friends. But she never thought of her as a typical imaginary friend; it was more practical when she thought of her as a sister. She would tell her why she was sad and why she was happy and have conversations about boys who chased her on the playground and boys who ignored her on the playground. Her "sister" would offer advice on what she should do to make this boy go away or that one notice her.

She even went to her imaginary sister for help in dealing with her parents. Angela often felt her mother was too hard on her about the clothes she wanted to wear or her dad was too strict with her on homework assignments. Once when she was ten years old and hadn't gotten the computer game she wanted for her birthday, she stormed into her bedroom, slammed the door, and got into an argument with her sister, who had somehow taken the side of her parents. After a long, sleepless night, she came to the realization that her sister was right and she was wrong. This had been a revelation. Angela knew from that day on that it wasn't just a little girl's game she was playing. It was an ongoing conversation with her conscience. Sometimes even a ten-year-old can see the truth through someone else's eyes.

So the sister she never had became the sister she invented, and to some extent she still talked to her today even as a nineteen-year old freshman. She didn't call her "Sally" the way she did when she was a little girl, but she talked to her in her head nonetheless. She would lay out her problems, and her conscience would review them and point out the pros and cons like a good friend or big sister often does. Sally/conscience would agree with her on the easy stuff but was surprisingly hard on her when it came to the big things that really meant something.

There had been a lot of those silent conversations that last year in high school when she was trying to decide if and where she was going to college. The "if" was pretty much a foregone conclusion where her mom and dad were concerned, but Angela had succeeded in keeping the "where" an open option. She had visited two different campuses with her mother and one with her dad, and each time she had brought the brochures home and studied them in conversation with her "sis." Distance from home was a big factor. She wanted to get as far away as possible, not because she didn't love her parents, but because she just felt it was the best way to start life on her own. But the other voice in her head had told her she might need the assurance of being only a couple hours away from everyone she knew and loved. Her sister, in the end, had won that argument. She was only three hours from Hanson. Far enough to be away—close enough to be home on Friday nights if she wanted to.

Majors were another big discussion. They had gone round and round on this one. What was she interested in? What would benefit her most? Where was she most likely to meet the right husband? What would give her more time for a social life on campus? What would require the most study? What would make her happy? When her heart and mind couldn't come to an agreement, she deferred the question until later. *Give it a year, and get used to the life.*

Today she wished her sister were real. Today she needed her not just for the decision-making help, but for the moral support—someone to stand beside her in what she was going to say, do. But Angela was on her own in this. There was no one else to blame. No one else to share the heat. What she was about to face, she would face alone.

$$\rightarrow$$

J. D. and Karlie were standing in the kitchen of their home on Circle Drive. They had decided to come home and eat a late lunch and do some book work in J. D.'s small office in the basement. The afternoon shift at the restaurant was intrigued and puzzled by the pieces of news trickling in about what had gone on in the Dining Club office an hour before, and before anyone asked them to explain, Karlie and J. D. decided to put a little distance between themselves and the curious. They would address the problem to those who needed to know in proper time.

J. D. was looking in the refrigerator while Karlie was going through the mail at the kitchen counter.

"Have you checked the phone messages?" J. D. asked with his head bent nearly to the bottom shelf as he reached for a carton of milk.

"No. I'll check in a minute." Karlie sounded distracted, as if she were reading something.

"You know, honey, I could feel bad about the outcome on a lot of different levels, but I also feel *good* about it on those same levels," J. D. said, straightening up with milk and mayonnaise in his hands. "Take Katherine, for instance."

"Katherine surprised me most," Karlie confessed. "I thought she would be the one who would calm the other two, and she turned out to be the one most offended by it all. She's been in this business much too long not to understand that sometimes things have to be done that are not pleasant."

"She surprised me, too. But she'll be all right by morning. To tell the truth, I expect to hear from her before the night's over. I'm betting she'll call. If she doesn't, I'll call her to make sure she's all right."

"That would be a good thing to do," said Karlie. "And I'll call Lottie. And should one of us call Crystal?"

"I suppose. But before we call anybody, we need to be real careful what we say. One of those women stole money from us and is probably celebrating having gotten away with it. Scared to death maybe, but celebrating at the same time. Maybe we don't want to call any of them. Maybe just let it be and see who comes in tomorrow."

Karlie turned and looked at her husband. "Are you suggesting that the one who doesn't come in is the guilty one?"

"Not necessarily. Could be exactly the other way around."

"Do you think it's down to two, or do you think it's possible that Crystal is still the one?"

J. D. measured what he felt in his heart about Crystal's convincing words, what he felt Caywood was thinking, and what he saw in her eyes and in the eyes of Lottie and Katherine as they stormed off the premises, and he changed his answer in his mind at least three time before it reached his lips.

"I'm ninety, ninety-five percent sure Crystal is telling the truth. I don't want it to be Katherine, and I'm probably leaning toward Lottie just because I don't know her as well as I do the other two and don't like her as well."

"Why don't you like her?"

"Well, for one thing...."

And at this they both turned as they heard the back door open and stood in total shock at seeing Angela coming in with a smile on her face that expressed little joy and plenty of apprehension. They both spoke the same words at the same time: "What are you doing here?"

→

Angela pulled a chair from the kitchen table and sat down, placing her oversized purse on the floor in front of her. She looked at the two of them and said, "Hi," feeling uncomfortable and trying to project confidence. Her parents waited in silence for her to answer their question.

"I decided to come home after all. Things are such a mess down there, and I just felt like I wanted to be here. I knew you'd understand."

"I'm not sure we do," said her mother. "How did you get here?"

"I came with a friend. Jenna. She's a junior and has a car. She comes home sometimes a couple of times a week."

"Jenna?" her father asked. "Do we know a Jenna?"

"Jenna Cummings. She's from here. Anyway, that doesn't matter. She was coming, so I hitched a ride with her."

"I thought you were staying to go to some sort of mixer this weekend. That's what you told me on the phone yesterday. What's changed?" Her father's tone sounded more suspicious than concerned.

"Yeah, I know I said that, and at the time I thought I would. But then I decided to come home. That's okay, isn't it?"

"Well, you're always welcome on the weekends, Angela. But it's the middle of the week. Are you missing classes? Because that's *not* okay." Her mother didn't even try to hide her irritation.

"Well, Mamma, yes, I'm missing classes. And you might as well know now I'm not planning on going back either."

"I beg your pardon?"

"I'm not planning on going back."

"*You're* not planning on going back … *you're* not planning on going back. And just when did this major decision become yours to make, young lady?"

"I don't know. College is not like I thought it would be, and I don't want to be there. I'll go back for the second semester the first of the year, but I need a break."

"A break! A break from what?"

"From school. I've been going to school for fourteen years. First preschool. Then kindergarten. Then first grade and middle school and high school, and I just need some time to myself before I take on college. Is that such a sin?"

"And what makes you so special?" her mother asked. "Isn't this what everybody does? They go to college. That's what they do. Didn't I do this and your father do this? Doesn't everyone you know do this? Are any of your other friends taking a 'break'?"

"I'm not everybody else." Angela looked at her father, who was still standing at the counter with the mayonnaise jar in his hand. "Make her understand, Daddy."

"Yeah, make me understand, Daddy," her mother said with fire in her voice and eyes.

$$\rightarrow$$

"All right, girls. I'm not sure what's going on here, but let's not lose it." J. D. said this to neither one in particular but turned his attention then to Angela. "You told me yesterday you wanted to stay at school. I was willing to let you come home for the weekend, but you said you *wanted* to stay at school. Is this about the girl getting attacked on campus?"

"No."

"Is it because you just don't like the school?"

"No."

"Then give me something here, Angela. There's got to be some reason why you're sitting here in our kitchen in the middle of the week only three weeks into the first semester. Are you scared?"

"Don't help her out, J. D. She'll come up with enough reasons on her own. Don't offer any."

J. D. turned his frustrations on his wife. "I wasn't offering anything. I'm just trying to find out what's going on."

An awkward silence fell over the room, and for a few moments no one said anything. J. D. and Karlie exchanged eye contact with very little message in it while Angela stared at the tiles on the floor as if counting the blocks in her mind. She was the first to speak.

"I haven't made any friends."

"What about Jenna, the girl who brought you home? Isn't she a new friend?" Karlie asked.

"I paid her ten dollars to give me a ride. She doesn't even know my last name."

There was another silence while J. D. and Karlie absorbed this and Angela found her voice again.

"It's not at all the way I always thought it would be. The way the brochures and the teachers and the guidance counselors said it would be. Everybody painted this bright and pretty picture and said how wonderful it was going to be to have new friends and roommates and how there would be parties, special events, and concerts and all that stuff. Well, I haven't seen any of that. And it's not the work. I don't mind the classes. I don't like them, but I don't mind them. And I never wanted to admit this, but I miss being at home. I miss my room. I miss Amy and Megan and Laura May. I miss Tommy, too. But not all *that* much. And I miss the both of you. I'm nineteen years old, but down there I feel like I'm thirteen. Remember the first night when you all left? It was a Sunday, and we had just unloaded all my stuff, and I stood on the parking lot and waved as you were pulling out. Well, I left there and went straight to my room. None of my suitemates were there, so I walked over to the cafeteria to get something to eat, and the place was almost empty. Seven o'clock on a Sunday night, and the ones who were there were paired off and laughing and having a good time—and then I spotted this one girl sitting by herself, reading a book. I went over and said, "Is it okay if I sit down here?" And she just kinda looked at me and said, 'Yeah.' So I did and tried to talk to her, and she was friendly enough, I guess. And then here comes this boy, and when she sees him she gets her book and stands up and says to me, 'See you later.' And as they were walking off she was telling him something, and they both laughed real big like I was some sort of goofus. I never felt more alone in my life. I wanted to call you right then and tell you to come back and get me."

Karlie started to say something, but J. D. held up his hand to stop her, and Angela continued staring at the floor tiles.

"I tried for the next couple of weeks, but it just didn't happen for me," Angela continued. "I saw other girls making friends, but it was like there was something about them that I just didn't want to be around. I called Megan and Amy a lot, but then they got to where they seemed busy and had to go every time I called. And then that thing Sunday night in front of the library. The girl got away, but they say she was beat up pretty bad. And I made up the thing about the mixer this weekend. There's going to be one, but I never planned to go."

"So what do you plan to do, honey?" Karlie asked with equal amounts of sternness and love in her voice.

"I want to stay here till next semester. Get a job. Maybe I could work in one of the restaurants the way I did in high school. Just let me have some time, and I'll work it out. Maybe even another school."

"What about the tuition we've already paid?"

"Oh, I knew money would enter into it somehow."

"Angela, be reasonable. You make a good argument, but your mother makes a good point."

"You both care more about the money than you do about me."

"Angela," Karlie scolded, "that's not true, and it's not fair to say that."

Angela grabbed her purse and slung it over her arm and headed for the door. "Don't worry about it. I'll go see Grandma. She'll understand. She cares how I feel."

As she stormed toward the door, Karlie warned, "Angela, don't you bother your grandmother with all this. And don't you ask her for any money."

But the door slammed before her last sentence ever reached Angela's ears.

$\rightarrow$

"Let her go. She'll cool down and Mom will be glad to see her, and we'll all sleep on it and work it out tomorrow." J. D. and Karlie both knew he was soft where his daughter was concerned and often gave in too soon and too often. But such are fathers and daughters. Karlie stood in the middle of her kitchen with her palms on her cheeks in exasperation. She sighed heavily and then turned and went up the steps toward the bedroom. J. D. threw what was still a half-made sandwich into the trashcan under the sink and walked across to the phone.

Pushing all the events of the day out of his mind momentarily, he clicked the button to retrieve the message indicated by the red light. "Mr. Wickman, this is Lavern Justice. Let's have coffee at your west-end restaurant real soon. I look forward to hearing from you."

Chapter Twelve

Angela didn't mind the atmosphere of Maple Manor as much as others her age did. She never dreaded visiting her grandmother the way her parents thought she would. Truth be known, she minded it a lot less than her dad did. She found a certain sense of comfort in the safety it provided and the available medical attention her grandmother never had when she was living in that big, old house of hers all alone. Going through the glass front doors and seeing the residents roaming the lobby in various stages of health was never a deterrent for her coming to see Grandma. The thought crossed her mind that maybe she should consider the nursing field. And maybe she would. There was time for that, too.

Angela walked through the lobby and twenty feet down the hall to the right and pushed the button for the smallest elevator she had ever been on. When the doors opened, she hoped it would empty all riders and that no one else would gather behind her while she waited for its descent. More than two on this shaky ride was a crowd. The doors parted almost immediately, and the car was mercifully empty. She stepped in and pushed the button marked "2," and after what seemed like at least a minute, the doors opened again and she was on her grandmother's floor. The second door on her right was marked "Beatrice M. Wickman." It was open, and the sounds of *General Hospital* were drifting into the hallway. As Angela entered the room, her grandmother reached for the remote control, switched off the set, reached out her arms, and said, "Baby."

After they hugged and cried a little, Angela sat on the side of her bed, held her hand, and said, "Well, aren't you going to ask me?"

"Ask you what, sweetheart? Why you cut your hair? I figured you just got tired of those pesky little bangs and just chopped 'em off!"

"No, Grandma," Angela said, nearly laughing. "Not my bangs. Aren't you going to ask me what I'm doing home?"

"But you're not at home. You're here visiting me. But if you want, I'll ask. What are you doing home, Angela?"

After nineteen years Angela still couldn't tell when Miss Beatrice, as she affectionately referred to her to other members of the family, was putting her on. She couldn't tell if her grandmother knew exactly what she was talking about and playing dumb, or if she just always saw the simple side of everything—or if she was still talking down to her as she did when she was a little girl. And Angela wasn't sure her dad knew either. Everyone, her aunts and cousins and her dad included, would just shake their heads at Beatrice's slightly askew take on life and say, "That's your grandma."

"I've quit school."

"Really?" Her grandmother looked genuinely puzzled and then added, "To do what?"

"What?" Now it was Angela's turn to be puzzled.

"You've quit school to do what? You must have had a plan."

"Yeah. I guess." Angela should have known better. She was expecting her to ask *why* she had quit school. But, "That's your grandma."

"I just want to get a job. Maybe work in one of the restaurants and then go back to school next semester. I'm just not ready to be in school again. I've been there all my life." She squeezed Beatrice's hand and looked her directly in the eye. "Are you going to tell me how silly I am too?"

"Is that what your father and mother told you?"

"In so many words, yes. They got pretty hot. Mamma more so than Dad, but both of them were pretty upset."

"They wanted a reason, didn't they?"

"Yeah, they did. And that's the hardest part. It's hard to explain. It's like … did you ever ride a bicycle, Grandma?"

"Yes, dearie. Believe it or not, they had bicycles back in the ice age when I was growing up."

"Then you know that feeling the first time you take off the training wheels? You're not scared. You're not frightened. Not really, anyway. But you've got this uneasy feeling in your stomach because you know you're going to eventually fall, and it's going to hurt. And you're just real shaky. It's that feeling in your stomach. Do you know what I mean?"

"Yes, I think I do. It's like walking into a room of people who all have been there and socializing before you. For a moment or two you're an outsider. It's like the first time you pray out loud in public. Or like what I felt that first night here at the Manor."

"You get it, Grandma. You always get it. That's what I'm feeling, and in three weeks it hasn't gone away and I don't think it is going to, because I just don't think the timing is right. I need the next couple of months to clear my head and get my mind ready. All I'm asking for is to just put it off till January."

"And your father and your mother are concerned about the money already spent that's not recoupable." This was more of a statement than a question, as if she already knew it to be true.

"You're exactly right! The money. That's what's bothering them." Angela's confidence was growing as she felt the family matriarch's support. But her grandmother's next response surprised her.

"And shouldn't it?"

"Huh?"

"Shouldn't it, sweetheart? It's not the first thing that's bothering them, I'm sure, but do you have any idea how much they have laid out for your first semester that they may never get back?"

"I have some idea."

"Do you really?"

"No. Not really."

"I didn't think so."

Angela's eyes scanned nervously around the room while Beatrice watched her. After a moment or two, her grandmother spoke again.

"Your parents were here yesterday morning. You dad is terribly worried about something."

"About what?"

"I'm not sure. But he has something weighing on his mind. I can always tell with him. When he's worried, his eyes droop. Whenever he gets tired or concerned, you can see it in his eyes. Have you ever noticed that?"

"I don't think so," Angela admitted.

"It's probably just a mother's instinct. 'Just a mother thing.' Isn't that what you all say?"

"Do you think he's sick?" Now her grandmother had her worried.

"No, he's not sick. Maybe heartsick in some way. Certainly worried and fretting over something. I'm not sure what, but I am sure it's something. I wish so often your daddy was a little more spiritual."

There was a pang in Angela's stomach that almost made her retch. What if it was she who was causing him to worry so much? Was she being selfish in not having thought about how this might bear on his mind? Just the thought that her actions might cause her father distress was more than she could bear. Was her grandmother seeing something she herself should have seen? Beatrice's voice brought her out of her reverie and back to Maple Manor.

"Don't be too hard on them, sweetie, until you've got all the facts. And while we're talking about all the facts, there are other things you don't know. Do you know that your father came home on his first Thanksgiving break from college and announced the very same thing to his father and me that you announced to him today?"

"You're kidding."

"Said he wanted to quit school and start all over the next year. He wasn't even considering the next semester. He wanted to quit until the next September."

"Why?" Angela was suddenly intrigued with this piece of family history she had never heard before.

"I'm not sure you're ready to hear why."

"Come on, Grandma. Quit teasing. Either tell me or not. And I prefer that you tell me because this is all news to me."

"Your daddy wanted to quit school and come home for a year so that.... No. I think I'd better not."

"Grandma, quit playing games. Please. Tell me."

"If I tell you, will you promise …?"

"Not to tell anyone?" Angela interrupted. "I promise not to tell a soul."

"No, that's not what I was going to say. If I tell you, will you promise to let those bangs grow out when you go back to school next week?"

Angela looked at her sweet face for a long moment before she realized how she was being manipulated. *But how can you lie to a grandma this cute?*

"I'll consider it," she promised. "Now tell me, please."

"Your father came home that first Thanksgiving and announced to the entire household, your aunts included, that he was not going back. When we pressed him for an answer, he fessed up pretty quickly with the truth. Your mother was, at the time, a senior in high school, and he was in love with her and wanted to wait on her so they could start college together."

"I never knew that. Why hasn't someone told me that story before? What happened? Did you make him go back, or did he quit?"

"That's not the point, honey. You want to know how it turned out so you can use the answer to your advantage. I'm telling you about this so that you will realize that someone, your father in particular, is aware of what you're feeling. Oh, you may not be in love with some young man you want to wait on, but your father understands that queasy feeling in your stomach. He had it too. So did I. Mine went away in a few days, and I stayed and endured it. So did your grandfather and your aunt Alice and your aunt Becky. Your daddy knows what you're feeling. We all do. Now, what you're going to do about it shouldn't be based on what he did about it. If I told you he waited, that doesn't mean you should do the same, and if I told you he went back to school after Thanksgiving, that doesn't mean you have to. All it says is that you're not the first to want to quit. You live with that much for a day or two, and then let's talk again."

The room was warm and cozy with the afternoon sun streaming in through the curtained window by the rolltop desk she used to color on in her grandfather's study. She was four or five in her earliest memory of her grandmother standing behind her and teaching her how to stay inside the lines with her crayons. There was a soft, familiar smell in the air—the signature sachet that Miss Beatrice still used. The hand Angela was holding was holding hers even tighter now.

Their eyes met and held for more than a second, and Beatrice Wickman looked lovingly at her granddaughter and said, "Do you ever watch any of the soaps in the afternoon at college?"

Angela had to laugh. "Yeah, actually I do. Just about every afternoon between classes."

"Let's watch one together," Grandma said. "We haven't done that for years."

→

"Do we wait dinner on her?"

"Not necessarily. She's with your mother. That'll be good for her. I say we let things be until tomorrow. Don't push it. She'll be home after while."

"I could call her on her cell."

"J. D., I just said I think we should let things take their course."

"Okay. You're probably right. It's nearly four thirty. I think I'll go back to the restaurant and see what the temperature is like there, and then I'll lock up tonight. Don't look for me till late."

J. D. went out the back door and thought how strange it was that neither of them said good-bye.

Chapter Thirteen

J. D. knew he would need to spend only about forty minutes at each restaurant. He hoped Karlie would expect him to take much longer because he had found no good time today to tell her that he and Jack were going out to Route 814 tonight. "Route 814" had become the euphemism in his conscience for going to the Clem house. It sounded saner inside his head. He could live with that. "Route 814" kept him from actually admitting to himself that he was visiting a family that was living sixty-five years ago. He knew he was only fooling himself to say he had not found a good time to tell Karlie what he and Jack were up to. He examined his rationalization for not telling her: It *had* been a full and eventful day beginning with the morning confession to Jack; then confronting Katherine and Lottie and Crystal this afternoon; and then being surprised by Angela's return and her announcement that she was quitting school. Still, he knew he should have told Karlie. The nerve ends in his stomach were jumping, and he was beginning to feel sick as he backed out of his driveway.

And then there was Lavern Justice. What did she want? What did she have to offer? He knew there would be no time to meet with her before he had to pick Jack up at six forty-five, but he could call her and make an appointment for tomorrow. No matter what they found tonight on Route 814, he still wanted all the information he could gather on the history of the Justice property.

All the employees at the downtown Dining Club were quiet and seemed to keep their distance as he asked normal questions about the day's business. They answered, but no one lingered to talk. It was all business, and he could feel the tension and discomfort in the air. He used the phone in the office to return Lavern Justice's call and got her answering machine. He told her tomorrow morning at ten would be a good time for him and if that didn't suit for her to let him know.

The crew at the west-end restaurant seemed less distracted, but he thought he could detect a little bit of distance in them also. Or maybe it was just his feelings of discomfort and not theirs. But all in all, things were moving along as expected in both restaurants and it was rapidly nearing six forty-five. He needed to check on Angela before he left, and he had two ways of doing that. He could call Angela directly and listen to all her one-sided gripes about life and how it was treating her and how unfair her mother was, or he could call Karlie and see if she had heard from Angela and risk having

Karlie ask him if he was going to be at one of the restaurants the rest of the evening. It took him a moment to decide which corner he wanted to be caught in.

"Hello?"

"Angela? Where did I catch you?"

"I'm at home."

"Is your mother there?"

"Yeah, she's in the kitchen. Do you want her?"

"No, silly. I called you. If I had wanted her, I'd have called the house. Did you go see Grandma?"

"Yeah, I did. We had a good time. She said to tell you hi."

"Well, good. What are you going to do tonight?"

"Just stay at home, I guess. That is, if Mom is talking to me."

"I'm sure she's talking to you. Has she ever let you down when you really needed her?"

"No."

And it wasn't until this one simple word that J. D. could detect tears in her voice. It broke his heart every time she cried, but he was glad she was showing the right emotion toward her mother. He decided to do the talking so she wouldn't feel embarrassed.

"Angela, you don't have to say another word. Just hang up and go in the kitchen and talk to your mother. Everything is going to be all right. I'll be home a little later, but if you two talk, I know things will work out."

"Daddy."

"Yes, honey."

"Can I ask you something?"

"Ask me anything you want. You know you can."

"Is something wrong? Grandma says there is."

"Wrong with who?"

"Wrong with you. She says she can tell when something's bothering you. She can see it in your eyes, and she knows you're worried sick about something."

There was silence on J. D.'s end of the line this time. His little girl had taken him by surprise—thanks to his mother and that old thing she always told everybody about his eyes drooping. He knew what was coming. He had to decide how to play it with her. He certainly wasn't going to tell *her* about Route 814. Now he was wishing he had taken his chances and called Karlie.

"Nothing for you to worry about, honey. Your mother and I have had some problems at the downtown restaurant we had to take care of today. You can ask her about it if you want to. Other than that, everything's fine."

"You sure, Daddy? You're not sick or anything, are you?"

"No, I'm not sick. Why don't you go talk to your mother and fix something to eat? I promise everything will be okay, and I'll see you later tonight."

"Okay, if you promise and say so."

"I promise and say so. And I love you."

"Love you, too, Daddy. Bye."

J. D. held the phone a long time before he placed it on the cradle. A lot of things were racing through his mind. But they were all mixed up. Angela and Lizzie and Crystal. Karlie and his mother and Jack. Paul and Ada Clem and Katherine Kimball and Lottie Arello. He wasn't sure what was real and what was a dream anymore. And what if all of it was real? Had the world changed from what he had always known it to be? And if some of it was a dream, then he just might be as crazy as Karlie and Jack thought.

He looked at his watch. He had five minutes to get to Jack's house.

$\rightarrow$

Jack's house was a small two-story brick home in the middle of a block of similar houses. He had owned other large, sprawling houses through the years—two others, to be exact—but this one was the final product of two marriages, two divorces, and too many alimony payments. He lived alone. There were no kids involved in any of the marriages—only money—and Jack always seemed to end up on the short end. He left his first wife for what the courts called "incompatibility," and that was a pretty accurate description. They had met at a Christmas party shortly after he went to work at Alden's drugstore. She, Alma Lee, was an X-ray technician, and they shared all the right interests. They loved to ski in the winter, sail in the summer, and catch all the latest movies at the Cineplex or little art theaters. But sometimes where that sameness can strengthen a relationship, it can also bore one or both of the parties to death. The latter prevailed, and in less than ten years, she got the house, and he got the sailboat.

Next came Florence, a virtual look-alike to Alma Lee. They both had auburn hair and long necks, and they could have been body doubles for one another. Jack and Flo shared none of the same interests, and this seemed to intrigue him to no end. He loved all the newness she brought to the relationship. He liked the fact that she knew more about football than he did, that she played the violin even though he couldn't stand the sound of it, and that she taught a yoga class he couldn't get the knack of. Their differences made the coupling interesting to him, but contentious for her. Again, in less than ten years, she got the house, and he got to sleep in the back of Alden's for nearly three months before he found the little house he now stood in front of, waiting for J. D. to pull up to the curb.

Jack got in the car, and neither of them spoke until they were well out of the city limits.

"Did you bring the penicillin?"

"I have it in my pocket."

Three more miles passed before either of them said another word. Jack couldn't stand it any longer.

"I don't know what I'm doing here. I feel like a complete idiot after that story you told me this morning. I mean, we have done some crazy things in our time, but this one borders on serious mental illness."

"Well, thank you. I appreciate those words of encouragement," J. D. shot back as sarcastically as possible.

"Come on, J. D. What do you expect? You've found the time machine? Do you know how ridiculous that sounds? And who are we going to see? A sixteen year-old girl in bed with septicemia?"

"If that means blood poisoning, yes."

"And who made you a doctor? What if there really is a kid out here who ran a nail through her foot? How do you know it's blood poisoning?"

"How do you know it's not until you look at her?"

"And that's something else. I told you I could lose my license giving you pills under the counter. Well, I could lose it just as easily prescribing medicine, you know. I can fill prescriptions, but I can't write 'em. And here you've got me going to hell and back with the intention of giving some girl illegal pills for her foot. How did I get into this anyway?"

"You can get out anytime you want. Just say the word, and I'll stop. But you leave the pills."

"What?"

"You heard me. You leave the pills."

"J. D., I do believe you're ready to fight me over this little matter. And I haven't seen you fightin' mad since our senior year in high school, at the homecoming football game when Gary Snead tried to kiss Karlie while everybody was cheering that final touchdown. You took him apart behind the bleachers and then"—Jack started to laugh—"and then he said"—laughing more—"he said, 'Don't hit me, and I'll give you ten dollars.' And you said, 'I already got ten dollars,' and you pulled back on him, and he ran like a monkey eatin' tacos."

They both laughed.

"And he was a head taller than you, and I know he outweighed you by thirty pounds. He was on the wrestling team, wasn't he?"

Their laughter turned into reminiscing, and it seemed like the old J. D. and Jack for the next fifteen minutes—until J. D. suddenly said, "It's less than a mile. What time you got?"

"Oh, seven fifteen. Seven seventeen to be exact."

"I'm going to slow down. If I've got this thing figured right, we need to hit the corner at precisely seven twenty. I know how that sounds, but I think it's important."

The car was quiet. J. D. kept a watch in his rearview mirror to make sure no car was coming up behind him. If it did, he was prepared to pull over and let it pass. He wanted to be the only vehicle on the road when they rounded the bend just before the one lane bridge.

"We're almost there, buddy," J. D. said, looking at his watch and seeing it hit 7:20 p.m. "It's just around this curve."

Jack was on the edge of his seat. J. D.'s jaw tightened, and beads of sweat formed on his brow. As they came out of the curve, the already slow-moving sports car came to a complete stop in the center of the road. Jack looked ahead and then to J. D.

"Is that it? Is that the bridge?"

J. D. was silent. After a long moment, he finally turned and looked his friend in the eyes. "That's a bridge, yes. But it's the *two* lane bridge. And that's Stan's One Stop on the other side of it."

Jack simply said, "What do we do now?"

"We go home."

"No," Jack protested. "Show me where the house was."

"It was right over there beyond that store."

"Let's go talk to the store owner."

"I already have. He doesn't know anything."

"Drive over there anyway. I want to see something."

J. D. drove slowly across the low-sided bridge and pulled into Stan's parking lot. Jack got out and walked around the car. J. D. got out and stood with him and rubbed his forehead with both hands.

"Is this the exact spot where the house was?"

J. D. looked behind him and said, "The lane came right up through there and the house was back where those cars are parked, and the front yard was here where the store is."

"Didn't you tell me when you broke down out here at their house that you didn't have any signal on your cell phone?"

"It was completely dead."

They pulled out their cell phones simultaneously, looked at them, and then looked at each other.

"Four bars," Jack said.

"Me too. I checked it before. I've checked everything you can possibly think of, and I can't figure out why I can come out here one time and that bridge is there and then come back and it's gone."

"Now don't take offense to this, J. D., but have you considered you might have suffered some kind of psychological lapse, or maybe you were in a dream state or a self-imposed trance or something of that sort?"

J. D. looked at his friend as if he had smacked him upside the head with a piece of wood. "Do you have any idea what you're talking about?"

"Well, no," Jack admitted, "but it makes as much sense as what you're spouting off at the mouth about. Look, I want to believe every word you're saying, but you have to give me something here. You have to give Karlie something too."

"Has she called you? Have you two talked about this?"

"No, but every time the phone rang today I was expecting it to be her. And it will be, I know for sure. And when she calls, I honestly don't know what I'm going to say. I'll cover for you in any way you want. You know that. But I don't know what I'm going to say."

"I know what she's going to say to you. She's going to ask you to talk me into seeing a doctor. I'll save you the call. I'm not going."

An old man in a sweatshirt and straw hat came out of Stan's One Stop and got in his truck. As he was about to pull off, he leaned out his window and said, "That a TR3?"

"Sure is," J. D. answered absently.

"What year? '62?"

"'61," J. D. said, this time with a friendlier smile.

"I used to have one almost exactly like that back when I was a young man. I lived down in Charlotte then. I had some good times in it. I ripped the roads and run through those gears slick as water through a funnel."

"It's a pretty good car," J. D. agreed.

"Brings back a lot of memories," the old man said, looking lovingly at the little machine from end to end. "Yesterdays are what keeps me alive. But you boys are too young to know what I'm talkin' about. You get to be my age, and you just live one day at a time. Yesterdays are sweet. Tomorrow—well, I figure I'll cross that bridge when I get there."

The two friends got back in the car and rode into Hanson in silence.

Chapter Fourteen

The house was quiet and dark except for a light in Angela's room and one in his and Karlie's room. It was after ten. He knew neither of them was asleep, but he came in quietly and took his cell phone off and plugged it into the charger on the kitchen counter. He got a Diet Coke from the refrigerator and walked upstairs. He found Karlie on the bed leafing through a *People* magazine from back to front, the way she always read it.

"How was everything at the restaurants?"

"Okay. A little strained, but okay."

"Have you been there all this time?"

He could lie to her and say yes or tell her the truth and say no and open up the whole subject all over again. For all he knew, she had talked to someone at both restaurants earlier in the evening and already knew he wasn't there the entire time. He had gone back to each after he dropped Jack at his house to lock up, but there certainly was a window from about six forty-five to eight fifteen he couldn't account for unless he told her the truth. And frankly, whether she *had* called the restaurants and checked on him didn't really matter at the moment. He simply needed her right now—her support, her understanding, and her help.

"I'll talk about that in a minute. How's Angela?"

"She's Angela. She'll be fine." Karlie smiled, still looking at her *People*.

"I called her this evening. Did she tell you?"

"Oh, yeah. She and your mother are worried there's something wrong with you." Now she looked up from her magazine. "Is there?"

"Nothing more than usual."

"You've been back out to that bridge, haven't you?"

"And I took Jack with me."

"So, what did he think?"

"The same thing you do. He thinks I'm loony and in need of a shrink. A 'psychological lapse,' I think he called it."

J. D. sat on the bed as if he were about to take his shoes off but didn't. Karlie reached over and rubbed the back of his neck.

"I know how you feel about all this," he said, "but I need a sounding board. I need to say out loud some of what's on my mind."

He turned and looked at her for a response, but all he saw was a concerned smile. Then finally she said, "Try me."

"Okay. I go for a ride in the country, and I come upon this family. I won't go into the details again because I know they upset you. But I run into this family, and then I come home and tell you about it. At your suggestion, we go back out there the next morning, and they and the bridge are gone. I've been thinking, 'What changed?' The first thing that hit me was the time of day. The first time was about seven twenty in the evening, and they were there. The next time was around eleven, eleven thirty the next morning. I even thought it might be the car. I was in the TR the first time, and we were in the van the next. So I thought the key had to be the time of day or the car. So I went back that same night, Tuesday night, at seven twenty in the van and I was able to cross over. So that told me it was the time of day and not the car. Do you follow me?"

"Don't ask me to agree with you or even understand. I'm your sounding board. Just talk."

"Okay. So now that I think I've figured out the key, Jack and I went back out tonight at exactly seven twenty and zip, nothing. So it's not the car *or* the time of day. And, honey, it's the time that has me concerned. One day passed on this side while two years passed on that side, and by the time I figure out how to cross over again, she may be dead."

"Who may be dead?"

"The girl. Haven't I told you about the nail in her foot and the blood poisoning?"

There was a long, chilling pause.

"J. D., you're scaring me all over again. What are you talking about?"

J. D. jumped up, as irritated at his wife's reluctance to understand as she was at his insistence to make her understand. She was crying and rolling her magazine into a tight tube that spoke volumes about what was going on inside her.

"I'm going downstairs. You go to bed, and we'll talk some other time."

"J. D., please. Please see someone about all this. Do it for Angela."

But he was gone down the steps and out the sliding-glass doors to the back patio. He sat in one of the lounge chairs and looked up at the stars. He had to make sense of all of this by himself because no one else was going to understand.

Lying there, staring at the stars with his mind racing, reminded him of countless summer nights he had spent in his backyard as a kid. He would sprawl in the grass on his back with his dog, King, on one side of him and Jack on the other, talking about the world and the future. A couple of ten-year-olds trying to understand the universe and all it held.

"Wouldn't you like to be able to fly?" J. D. once asked innocently.

"Not me. My daddy says if God meant for man to fly, everybody would be born without luggage."

"What's that mean?"

"I don't know, but he always says it, and everybody laughs real big."

"I wouldn't want to be an astronaut. That'd be too scary. Maybe a jet pilot."

"Do astronauts have stewardresses?"

"You mean stewardesses."

"Whatever."

"Naw. But jet pilots do." And they both laughed loudly and heartily enough to make King bark one sharp yip as his contribution.

"Do you think if you got on a spaceship you could fly into the future?" Jack asked with all the sincerity of his age.

"Maybe. Or maybe back into the past."

"Boy, that would be cool! Where would you want to go?"

"You first," J. D. countered. "Where would you want to go?"

Jack thought on it a minute and then said slowly, as if choosing words that were going into some sort of proclamation, "I'd like to go back to the Old West. To an old western town like on *Gunsmoke*. Meet Wyatt Earp and Wild Bill Hickok and Matt Dillon."

"Matt Dillon ain't real."

"Yes, he is."

"No, he ain't. Wyatt Earp and Wild Bill Hickok are real, but Matt Dillon is made up."

"Well, I'd still like to meet him." Jack held his ground. "What about you? Where would you like to go? Or do you want King to go next?"

They both laughed really big at this joke too, and Jack reached across J. D. and rubbed the old dog's head when he barked again at the sound of his name. All three settled down, and after a minute of real contemplation, J. D. said, "I'd like to go back and meet my grandfather. He was a preacher, and everybody tells all kinds of neat stories about him. He died before I was born. He died in the war. World War II. So I'd like to go back sometime before he died just to see what he was really like."

"Was he real religious?"

"I said he was a preacher. Of course he was religious."

"But I mean did he pray all the time and stuff?"

"Yeah, I reckon. Not all the time maybe. Some of the time he was shootin' people in the war. And then he got shot."

"Speakin' of shootin' people, have you ever noticed in *Gunsmoke* how at the start of every show Matt Dillon is out in the street, and he and the bad guy draw and shoot and the bad guy beats him to the draw and shoots first, but then Matt Dillon shoots him? I think it's weird how the bad guy actually outdraws him."

"You're just eat up with Matt Dillon."

"You like him too."

"Yeah, but not like you do."

And then the conversations would go on and on, and the nights would weave into late summer, and the talks in the grass evolved to talks in their cars as they circled the town square as teenagers. And then to the all-night coffee shops during college. They never tired of trying to decipher the mysteries of the universe and the wonders of the world around them. And they always did it together. Just as they were trying to do now in finding the secret to the latest enigma in their lives. But this one wasn't really theirs. It was all J. D.'s, and he was becoming more and more aware of that fact with each passing hour. He couldn't share it with Jack or with Karlie. They hadn't experienced it. They couldn't know what it meant to him, what he was feeling. Not like the many things they had shared together. And with these thoughts running wildly through his head, he almost fell asleep until something from deep inside jarred him unmercifully awake.

He had it! He knew the code! He locked the glass doors and ran for the car.

Chapter Fifteen

Midnight on a country road is dark. No street lights. No passing headlights. No neon signs. Just a heavenly quiet with shadows from the atmosphere of God's perfect nature. J. D. sat on the hood of his little green Triumph, basking in the serenity of it all. The moon and the stars reflected off the silvery steel of the one lane bridge. In the distance he could see just the outline of two chimneys from the old farmhouse behind the rising hill. It was too late to pay a visit, but that didn't bother him now because he knew he could come back.

He wasn't aware how long he had been sitting there; he only realized that he was smiling from somewhere down in his soul. This was *his*. All his, and no one else could help him. The only way for him to cross over was to be alone. Not with Karlie or Jack or a doctor or anyone else. Alone was how he had to handle this, and he was up to the task of doing whatever it was he was supposed to do. He now knew the "what" and the "how." Maybe later, God willing, he'd learn the "why."

PART II

Chapter Sixteen

The phone rang at 6:30 a.m. J. D. usually got it before the second ring, but this morning it sounded so very far away. He couldn't figure out where the noise was coming from, and he heard it blast at least three times before someone finally silenced it. That someone was Karlie, reaching over him from her side of the bed and picking up the receiver from the nightstand.

"Hello. Yes. All right. All right. All right. That'll be fine. Thank you. Good-bye."

J. D. lay with his eyes shut, waiting for her to put the phone back on the table, but she never did. She had apparently just hit the off button and was sitting against the headboard with it still in her hand.

Putting his arm wearily across his eyes to block out any semblance of daylight that might be leaking through the blinded windows, he said, "One of the restaurants?"

"Yeah."

"Don't tell me. Lottie didn't come in."

"No. Lottie is in. That was her on the phone. And Crystal is there. Katherine didn't come in."

Now he allowed himself a peek from the corner of his eye and saw the strange and puzzled look on his wife's wide-awake face.

"What's that say to you?" he asked.

"Could mean anything. Could go either way."

J. D. stared across the room at the blank TV screen at the foot of their bed and then rubbed his eyes with both hands. "Don't forget what the Godfather told Michael."

"I beg your pardon?" Karlie said with more than a hint of concern.

"The Godfather told Michael that the guilty one would be the one who made contact with him. He said, 'Whoever approaches you, whoever gets in touch with you, that's your guilty man.' And it was Fish."

"Abe Vigoda," she corrected.

"Yeah," J. D. continued, "Fish was the one who came to him after the funeral and suggested they have a meeting, and he was the guilty one."

"And what does all this have to do with our situation?"

"I'm not sure, but it's good to see you smile at me again."

Karlie threw the covers back and got out of bed, saying, "Well, if I was smiling, I apologize. And what are you so chipper about this morning anyway? You didn't come to bed till two o'clock."

"I found some peace in all this, Karlie. Let's not talk about it right now because it always goes off in the wrong direction and we wind up on opposite ends, and I just don't want to be on the outs with you right now. I need things to be right, so let's just agree not to talk about it. I think I'll be able to explain it soon."

Karlie asked, "Are you going in early this morning, or do you want me to?"

"I'll handle both places. You call Katherine and see what's eating her. She always liked you better than she did me anyway."

$$\rightarrow$$

As J. D. showered and shaved, his mind raced with all he had to do. First up was the meeting with Lavern Justice at ten o'clock. He wasn't sure why he was so nervous about that, but there was something about the woman that set him on edge. She was friendly enough but spoke with an air of authority and superiority that made him uneasy. But she had called *him*, so why should he even worry about her? And anyway, that wasn't what was foremost in his mind. The most urgent thing this morning was to find a way to get a bottle of penicillin to the Clem house. He could beg Jack one more time, but in his heart he knew that was useless. He could go to his family doctor and fake some kind of illness, but last night he had exhausted every possible scenario he could think of and hadn't come up with the right sort of deceitful story that would bag him the goods he needed. His best chance was his dentist. He could fake a toothache and hope for the best. The hardest thing would be getting an appointment. He would have to make it sound like a real emergency.

J. D. was at the downtown restaurant by seven thirty to help Lottie and Crystal at the tables and do a few things in the kitchen that Katherine ordinarily would have done. He asked them what they knew about Katherine's failure to show up, and they both insisted they had not talked to her since she left the building yesterday afternoon. Lottie said this was not unusual as they didn't normally socialize outside of work, and Crystal just shrugged her shoulders. This concluded the extent of their conversation for the hour and a half he was there.

Just before leaving, he went in the little office and closed the door. He looked up the number for Dr. Howard Carnham and dialed.

"Hello, Dr. Carnham, DDS."

"Hello. Who is this please?"

"This is Cheryl."

"Cheryl, this is J. D. Wickman. I'm a patient of Dr. Carnham's."

"Oh, yes, Mr. Wickman. How are you this morning?"

"Well, that's why I'm calling. I've got a little problem, and I was wondering if you could work me in sometime this morning."

"And what exactly is the problem?"

"I'm not real sure. It's a terrible toothache. It's really not swollen all that badly, but it's real sore to the touch, and I'm afraid to let it go any longer."

"How long has it been bothering you, Mr. Wickman, and what tooth is it?"

"It's been going on for a couple of days now, and it's in the back on the upper right hand side."

"Dr. Carnham could see you at four fifteen this afternoon."

"Nothing sooner?"

"I'm afraid not. He's not in today until after lunch, and then he has three extractions. Four fifteen is the earliest he could possibly see you."

"Okay then. Four fifteen it is, and thank you."

"Thank you, Mr. Wickman, and have a nice day."

Shortly after nine he arrived at the west-end restaurant, and after forty-five minutes at his desk he looked at his watch and realized Lavern Justice would be there soon. He fixed a decanter of coffee and set two cups in the back booth against the wall, the one farthest from the front door. It was the most private table on the floor, and he had a feeling privacy was going to be of the utmost importance.

At precisely ten o'clock she walked in the door and straight toward him. She looked smaller than she had in her living room. She was dressed in tan slacks and a leather jacket that looked too heavy for the season. She smiled as he rose; she shook his hand with a firm confidence and sat down with no further invitation.

"I see you have coffee ready and waiting. You read my mind."

"I thought you looked like a coffee drinker. It's a little game I play with myself. I can tell when a customer walks in the door if they're a coffee drinker or a Coke or iced-tea drinker. And more and more, just plain water drinkers. Used to be, people were ashamed to ask for just water. Afraid they'd appear cheap. Now they do it with pride to show how health conscious they are."

Lavern laughed and agreed and made some comment about how times have changed, then let the conversation crawl to a standstill and just stared across the table at her young host.

"We have a lot to talk about, J. D. Wickman."

"Do we?" he asked with equal amounts flippancy and sincerity. "You're the one who called me, so I figured you had something to tell."

"Two days ago when you came to see me, I felt there were unresolved issues when you left. That maybe you had more you wanted to say."

"Not really." J. D. didn't lie. There was more to say, but he wasn't sure he had wanted to say it. But this woman was not about to let a thread hang without tugging at it.

"You're not doing family tree research, J. D. And I doubt if your grandmother ever lived in the state, much less the county. So what's it all about, and why do I find you so interesting?"

"I'm not sure I can answer that one for you. But while we're asking questions, why are you so dead sure I'm lying to you? I only came by your house because a girl at the courthouse said you might have some background."

"That's part of it. You came by the house. It was urgent for you. You didn't call or write or email. You came straight from the courthouse. It's as if time was important. And time is not important to a family tree."

"I think you're seeing more in this than is there, Ms. Justice. Maybe you just don't like me—I rub you wrong—and you're trying to pick me apart."

"On the contrary. I like you very much, J. D. That's why I called you yesterday. I think I can help you."

"Wonderful!"

Lavern Justice squinted across the table at him and said in her lowest and severest tone yet, "You be honest with me, and I'll be honest with you."

J. D. said nothing. He just studied her countenance. She was a serious and deeply concerned woman. She had something to say, and he felt his silence would best draw her out. Sparring with her would only prolong the inevitable. He smiled at her and gave her the floor.

"Have you ever heard of a Truth Light, Mr. Wickman?" she asked as he poured her a second cup of coffee."

J. D. shook his head but said nothing.

"I've known a few people in my life who have what is called a Truth Light. It's a light that shines in the corner of your eye. Very dim. Unobtrusive. But whenever someone lies to you, that light gets brighter and brighter. Sometimes it's so bright it's blinding. My dear old aunt Mandy in Ohio had the Light. And I've had a few friends in my lifetime who have had the same gift. It's, let's say, a lie barometer. It's quite useful sometimes and quite annoying at other times."

"And you have this light?"

"I do. And it's very faint and weak today. But two days ago when you were in my den, it was like a sunrise after a week of rain. I could hardly hold my eye open."

"Are you some sort of psychic, Ms. Justice?"

"Oh, no, nothing like that. It's all spiritual. I'm very spiritual, as a matter of fact."

She looked at J. D. a long time before speaking again. He wanted to say something but wasn't sure how serious this conversation had gotten. But he was about to find out.

"Are you a man of faith, J. D.?"

"I go to the Presbyterian chu—"

"I didn't ask you if you went to church, J. D.," Lavern Justice interrupted. "I asked if you were a man of faith. Two entirely different questions."

"Okay then. The answer is yes."

"You have faith because you go to church?"

"No, I go to church because I have faith."

"Good answer!" Lavern said as she threw her head back and roared out a laugh. But the laugh was gone as quickly as it came. She reached over and put her hand over his in a motherly fashion and said in a near whisper, "What's going on, J. D.? You need someone you can trust, and I don't know how to convince you of it, but I'm that someone. There's nothing you can tell me I haven't heard before. I'm not going to scoff at you or tell you you're crazy. And if I can't help you, I'll tell you that, too. But right now I sense—I *know*—that you need someone."

J. D. took time to absorb the words she had just spoken to him. He took so much time that he was suddenly aware that he wasn't even uncomfortable keeping her waiting for an answer. And she wasn't either. They both seemed to understand that these things took time, and there was comfort and understanding between them even in silence.

"Have you ever seen something that wasn't there?" he asked as his opening feeler question.

"No. If you see it, it's there. Think of it as dimensions. Not illusions."

"I passed over a one lane bridge and was taken back in time. Back sixty-five years to that house your father owned. I met the family that lived there. One of them, a young girl, is sick, and she needs a medicine that wasn't available at the time. And I'm the only one who can save her life."

"Penicillin?"

"How'd you know that?"

"It isn't hard to guess. Sixty-five years ago. It was quite a miracle drug when it came out. Still is, truth be known. But it was a big discovery about that time."

"I need to go back out there, and I need to take her the medicine."

"Do you need me to go with you?"

"I don't think I can take you. I'm not really sure how this works … but … I think this is something only I can do. I suppose that makes me sound even crazier, but I don't think I can cross over when someone else is with me. I know how that must sound...."

"I understand. How can I help?"

"I need the drug."

Lavern reached in her purse and pulled out a pencil and paper and began writing while J. D. continued talking.

"My wife and best friend think I'm crazy. They want me to see a doctor, and the only doctor I'm willing to see is one who can get me a bottle of penicillin."

"Why do you think this will work? Is there infection?"

"Yeah. Nail through the foot."

Lavern handed him the slip of paper. It had a name and address on it. The address was for a town twenty miles east, and the name was a Dr. Navin Annata. He read it and then asked, "Who is this?"

"He's the man who can help you. Trust me."

"Just what sort of doctor is he? And who … what are you?"

"J. D., you insult me. Call us spiritualists if you like. But know that we're God-fearing and caring. We believe what you believe and maybe a little more. Let's just say we're willing to go the extra mile others often aren't."

"So when do I see this Dr. Annata?"

"As soon as you can get there."

"Do I need an appointment?"

"As soon as you can get there," she repeated as she rose to go.

"One more question, Ms. Justice. The light in your eye. What's it look like right now?"

"As dim as a quarter moon on a cloudy night. Now hurry. You may not have much time."

Chapter Seventeen

Karlie and Angela had a quiet breakfast of toast and orange juice. *The Today Show* was on but not loudly enough to hear the news. They didn't say a word about the college. Karlie was making an honest effort to give her daughter a conflict-free weekend and wait to talk with her when they were both of a cooler mind. They laughed and enjoyed each other's company, and it looked like a good day was being born right in front of their eyes. Angela had just gone upstairs to shower and Karlie had walked over to the phone to dial Katherine on J. D.'s suggestion when someone knocked at the back door. Karlie opened it to find a very tired and weary-looking Katherine Kimball standing on her back porch.

"Katherine! Come in."

"Thank you. I won't stay, but I felt we needed to talk."

"You know we can always talk. Do you want some coffee?"

"I've had plenty already this morning. Are you alone?"

"Angela's here. She's upstairs."

"She's not at school?

"No. It's a long story and kind of a mess. I'll tell you about it some other time. Come on and sit down."

"Karlie, I've always liked you so very, very much. I think you know that. And I've loved my job from the very first day. We've never had a cross word. Not between you and me or J. D. and me. It's been just a perfect relationship."

"Katherine, let me just say that we …"

"No, please, Karlie. Let me talk before I lose my nerve. I can't tell you how nervous I was coming here this morning. I didn't go into work because I didn't know if I should or not. I didn't know if I was fired or if I still worked there. So I just didn't go in, and then I got to feeling so bad I felt like I needed to come here and just talk to you and get some things said."

"I'm glad you did. And no, you weren't fired. You know better than that."

"Well, I was pretty upset when I left there yesterday afternoon. I felt like I had been accused of being a thief."

"We were doing what we had to do."

"But why couldn't you have come to me and told me what you were doing? Did you really think I was the one?"

"We couldn't be sure. Can't you understand that?"

"No, I can't. I can't believe that you thought for a second that I would steal from the two of you. You're like a son and daughter to me, and I was just so hurt when I saw you put me in the same pocket as Lottie and Crystal. They're good girls, but I've been with you so long. I guess I thought I meant more to you than that."

"You do, Katherine. You do. So right now you're telling me you think it's either Lottie or Crystal?"

"I guess it has to be."

"Then how would you suggest we proceed? I'm asking you now the way you wanted to be asked. What would you do that wouldn't offend the one that's innocent?"

"I'd talk to them one at a time and see how they react."

"We could have done it that way, but then by the time we talked to all three of you, it's likely the guilty party would have been warned. Maybe we could have done it differently and better. We did the best we could with the time we had to do it. And we're sorry you're offended or hurt. But if you're innocent, you shouldn't be offended."

"*If* I'm innocent. You still don't believe me, do you?"

"You still haven't said you're innocent. Do you want to look me in the eye and assure me that it wasn't you who took the money?"

"Do I have to do that in order for you to believe me?"

"Yes, you do."

"You didn't find the money in my purse, did you, Karlie?"

"No, we found it in Crystal's, and she said it had been planted there."

"So where do we stand?"

There were no tears in the offing on either side of the conversation. It was all a very matter-of-fact confrontation, and neither side was giving quarter. Katherine Kimball was protecting her pride or her dishonesty, and Karlie Wickman was defending her position and her authority. Both women took stock of the other one the way master poker players might eye an opponent from behind their hands. The question of "where do we stand?" was never answered as the scene was disrupted by Angela bouncing down the steps, wrapped in a towel.

"Mrs. Kimball! What are you doing here?"

Angela hugged Katherine, and Katherine gave her a scolding look and said, "What are *you* doing here, girl? Shouldn't you be in school?"

"Yeah, I guess." Angela laughed self-consciously.

"Well, I was just going. I have to get out of here." As she started toward the door she leaned back to Angela's ear. "I don't know what's going on, but I know your mother's worried sick over you." Then to Karlie she said, "I'll talk to you later. Maybe tomorrow. You have a nice weekend."

"You do the same," Karlie said and then closed the kitchen door behind her.

$\rightarrow$

J. D. drove the twenty miles east to Corban Springs and found the address Lavern Justice had written out for him. It was a small brick building on the edge of a strip mall lined with insurance and mortgage offices. There was parking near the front door. He went inside and found behind the reception desk a heavyset, round-faced woman who smiled at him and asked him his name.

"J. D. Wickman."

Scanning her appointment screen, she said, "Wickman. Wickman. What time was your appointment, Mr. Wickman?"

"I really didn't have a set time. It was just made by phone a little while ago."

"And who did you make it with?"

"I'm not sure. I didn't actually make it myself. A Ms. Justice called it in, I think, and I don't know who she might have talked to." He dropped his voice and said, "I'm supposed to pick up a prescription for penicillin."

Looking past her, J. D. counted nine nurses-receptionists-assistants milling around from desk to desk among the filing cabinets. There were more people on her side of the glass than there were on his, and the waiting room was almost full.

"Have a seat, Mr. Wickman, and someone will be with you momentarily."

He had only been seated a minute, just long enough to glance at the seven other people who were in the waiting room, when a woman in a pink pullover and gray slacks, presumably a nurse, came out and called his name. Every head in the room turned to watch his departure with a scowl. The pink nurse ushered him into a small treatment room and he sat down in a straight-backed chair as she stood in the doorway. She assured him with a smile that the doctor would be in momentarily, then closed the door behind her. He looked around at the charts on the wall explaining blood pressure readings and artery blockage and the insides of the human torso. He picked up a short stack of magazines consisting of *Health Today* and *Progressive Wellness* and tried to find something to read to pass the minutes. He finally decided on a well-worn *Newsweek,* but after leafing through a few pages, he turned back to the front cover and discovered it was three and a half years old. He only hoped doctors were more particular in keeping their medical magazines updated than their news.

After about ten minutes, two short raps at the door announced that someone was about to enter. The door opened, and a short, dark man of indeterminate nationality walked in, wearing a crisp white jacket over a blue open-collar shirt. His thin black hair was receding, and he wore thick red-rimmed glasses.

"I'm Dr. Annata." His accent was thick and his speech was clipped, and J. D. immediately began worrying if he was going to be able to communicate with him. They shook hands while the doctor held a clipboard in his left.

"I'm J. D. Wickman."

"Yes. I have your name. You are here for medicine."

"Yes. Did Ms. Justice talk to you?"

"Ms. Justice." The way the doctor said her name, J. D. couldn't tell if he was asking a question or merely repeating what he had just said.

"Ms. Justice," J. D. said to add clarity.

"Ms. Justice. Ms. Liberty. Mount Rushmore."

J. D. stared at the doctor. He wasn't sure if he was supposed to laugh at or ignore this little exchange. J. D. wondered if he needed to make up a malady—or had it all been prearranged. Finally, out of desperation, he said to Dr. Annata, "What do you need from me?"

"I need nothing. Nothing. You need something from me. Are you sick?"

"Well"—J. D. hesitated—"I have felt better in my time."

"Something hurts you, yes?"

"Yes, you could say that. I wasn't given a lot of information before I came here, but you apparently knew I was coming so you must know what this is all about."

"About? I know nothing about nothing. What your name?"

"My name's Wickman. J. D."

"What your drugstore?"

"Any one you want. I'll go wherever you want me to."

"How much you weigh?"

"One hundred seventy-eight pounds. Why? What's that got to do with it?"

"American citizen?"

"Yes, but I don't understand...."

"Caportab?"

"I beg your pardon. I don't understand what you're saying."

"Caportab?"

"Capsule or tablet? Is that what you're saying?"

"Yah. Caportab?"

"Oh. I don't care. Either."

"Amoxicillin. Give you twenty-eight. Don't stop till all are gone."

"Yes sir."

"Fifty dollar."

"You want it now?"

"Fifty dollar." And the doctor held out his hand.

Dr. Navin Annata handed him a small piece of white paper with ink scrawling on it and then turned and was gone as quickly as he came. J. D. could hardly believe it. After all the worrying and the scheming, apparently it only took a single phone call from Lavern

Justice, and it was done. The medicine was only a drugstore visit away from being in his hands. Who was Lavern Justice, and what was her connection? And who was Dr. Annata to her? He would find out in time, or maybe he would never find out. Right now, it didn't really matter. He only hoped he could get it to Lizzie in time.

Chapter Eighteen

Spartan's Drugs was in the same strip mall as the doctor's office. He walked over and waited while they filled the prescription. He paid for it in cash and, while walking back to his car, looked at his watch. It was 12:35. He could be at Route 814 in forty-five minutes. He considered calling Karlie but thought better of it. It was better she didn't know his every movement where this situation was concerned. He did want to make one stop, though. He pulled up to the Safeway grocery across the street to buy some more essentials to take with him. He wasn't sure how much time had passed since his visit two days ago, but he was certain Paul and Lizzie could use some more food. He thought again about the fact that two years almost to the day had passed between his first two visits. If that pattern held true, he was already too late. He could only hope and pray that another two years had not passed. Or if it had, that Lizzie had survived. Thinking about how the time worked only hurt his head. None of the calculations he tried in his head made reasonable sense, but then, nothing about this whole thing made sense. He bought bread and milk and vegetables and considered for a moment buying them a newspaper but was unsure what sort of effect that might have on the whole matter. By 1:00 p.m. he was on the road.

$\rightarrow$

The closer he got to his destination, the more unsure he became. His hands were sweating on the steering wheel, and the air conditioning was making him clammy instead of cool. He took a deep breath but could do nothing to slow his heart pounding in his chest. He turned the radio off because the music was more annoying than soothing, interfering with the wild thoughts rushing through his mind.

The road began to turn to the left as the sun bounced off the windshield and blinded him for a second. When he realized it had blinded him because it was reflecting off the steel beams of the one lane bridge, he whispered a three-word prayer: "Thank You, Lord." As he crossed the bridge, he realized he had a smile of relief on his face, and then as he turned up the dirt lane to the house and con-sidered what he might actually find, the smile bent into a sickening frown. What if Lizzie was dead? What if the Clem family no longer lived there? What if it was another time altogether and not 1942?

There was a queasy, uneasy feeling in his stomach, and he felt less sure of the situation than he ever had.

He pulled next to the old cistern beside the house and turned off his engine. It took every ounce of strength and courage he could conjure up to open the door and step out. The yard was dusty around scattered patches of tall grass. He walked to the back screen door with the grocery bags in his hands and knocked. He was about to go around to the front door when he heard movement inside. A figure he could hardly detect through the screen pushed open the door with squeaky hinges and said, "Hello."

It was Paul.

"Mr. Clem. Do you remember me?"

He didn't say anything immediately. He just looked J. D. up and down as if trying to register a proper answer.

"I remember you."

"I was here before and brought you some groceries."

"That's right. What can I do for you?"

"Well, sir, I have some more food, and I wanted to check on Lizzie. How is she?"

Paul Clem stood in the doorway, offering no invitation to come in. He eyed J. D. coldly, and when he did finally speak, it was hard to find a hint of warmth in any of his words.

"Lizzie is a sick little girl."

"May I see her?"

"Who are you exactly? And why do you keep coming here?"

"My name is Wickman, and to be honest with you, sir, I'm not sure why I keep coming here. But I think it's because I can help. I can help Lizzie."

"How?"

J. D. knew the wrong word or the wrong tone could mean losing the moment forever. Paul was on the verge of kicking him off the property. J. D. didn't want to irritate or anger Paul because there was no way he was going to allow himself to be sent away after having come this far. He chose his words carefully.

"I have food and medication I think will help her. If you'll let me see her I may be able to make her well."

"You a doctor, Wickman? Or some kinda county relief worker?"

"No. But trust me, Mr. Clem. I can help her. What do you have to lose by letting me try?"

Paul Clem didn't answer his question. At least not out loud. After a few moments of consideration, he stepped back and held the door for J. D. to walk past him.

J. D. set the bags on the kitchen table. He looked toward the living room, but it was dark, as if every shade in the house had been pulled. He looked back to Paul standing behind him and asked permission to go to Lizzie by simply raising his eyebrows. Paul, in return, nodded his approval and began taking the groceries from the plastic bags as J. D. pushed his way through the beaded doorway.

J. D. whispered softly as he entered the darkened living room, "Lizzie. Lizzie, it's me. John Wickman. Are you awake?"

She didn't answer, but he could hear movement from the far corner. Then a lamp switched on, and he could see the small, frail figure of a blonde-haired girl lying on yellowed sheets. Her hair was glued to her head from the heat, and her face was a mixture of sleep and pain. But through all this she smiled at him and said, "John Wickman. You came back."

"I did, Lizzie. How are you feeling?"

"Kinda weak. My leg hurts a lot. And my foot."

"Can I see your foot?" he asked, frightened at the thought of what he might find.

"Sure," Lizzie said, pulling back the sheets to expose her swollen right foot.

It was much bigger than it had been two days ago, and it had turned from a pink to a yellowish red. He had always heard that red streaks would run up the leg if it was blood poisoning, and to his uneducated eye he was sure he could see signs of that. He didn't touch it for fear of hurting her. Instead he pulled a chair up to the bed and sat down so he could speak to her in something lower than conversational tones.

"Lizzie, do you have a glass of water in here?"

"Sure," she said, reaching toward a table on the other side of her bed. "You want a drink?"

"No, but I want you to take this pill."

He reached in his pocket and pulled out the small bottle of amoxicillin and removed the childproof cap. He shook a tablet out into her hand and watched as she put it to her lips and drained the half-full glass of water. She never questioned what she was taking or why. She totally trusted his authority as she probably did any adult.

"You have to take one of these every six hours. Do you have a watch?"

"No, but there's a clock over there on the mantle. It was Grandma Clem's. I get it whenever something happens to Daddy."

"Okay. Now you keep an eye on the time, and you take one of these again at eight o'clock tonight. And Lizzie, let me show you about this top. It's a little tricky to work. You have to push down on it and turn it to the right. Here, you try it."

"I never seen anything like this. Where'd you get this?"

"At the drugstore. It's … it's a new kind of bottle. A safety bottle. Do it again to make sure you know how."

Lizzie did it five or six times, as if playing a game she enjoyed. J. D. took the bottle from her and placed it on the table by her bed. He looked at her pale complexion and gaunt features and felt lost for the proper words to say to her. There was one nagging question in his mind, though, and he knew no better way than to just ask.

"How long since I was last here, Lizzie?"

"Don't you know?"

"I think so. Was it two days ago?" He held his breath.

"Look at that calendar on the back of the door. I think it's the thirteenth. I know it's Sunday. See if it ain't Sunday the thirteenth, and I think you were here three days ago."

He walked to the door and looked at the Conner's Insurance calendar, which had a picture of the Grand Canyon for September. Lizzie was right. It was Sunday, September 13, 1942. Only three days had passed since his last visit. Two years between his first two visits and only three days since his last. Where was the rhyme and reason? But now the days were properly lined up for some purpose beyond his comprehension. It was September 13 on both sides of the bridge. Exactly sixty-five years apart. Sunday afternoon on one side and Thursday afternoon on the other. Did this mean something, or was he trying to make too much of it all? Was every little detail supposed to add up to something important? Or was it just God's way of keeping him off balance and in the dark? Another of those "mysterious

ways" He enjoyed moving in? J. D. could make no sense of it. But all
that really mattered was that time had slowed down enough for him
to get Lizzie the cure she needed. He hoped, prayed it worked. He
would have to come back to find out, and he was already plotting his
next visit when he heard Lizzie talking to him.

"Do you think I'm going to die?"

"No, I don't, Lizzie. I think you're going to be just fine. But
it's very important you take all these pills. You will do that, won't
you?"

"You think I'll die if I don't, don't you?"

"I think … you might have if we hadn't gotten those pills to
you."

"I don't want to die. I lay here at nights and think about dying
and how there's just nothing. You're dead and you lay in a cemetery
forever and ever in the ground, and that scares me."

"Don't think those kinds of thoughts, Lizzie. You're going to be
okay. Do you go to church anywhere?"

"Sometimes. Sometimes me and Daddy go to the Four Square
Gospel Church. Mamma used to go all the time. We don't go much
anymore. I don't think he likes church people very much."

"Did you learn about heaven at that church?"

"Some. But me and Daddy don't believe in heaven very much."

"Why's that?"

"Well, Daddy says if you can't see it and can't touch it, it ain't
there. And that makes sense to me, too."

"Lizzie, you can't see and touch a lot of things, but they're there
none the less."

"Like what?"

"Well, like the wind. Or the dark. Or the cold. Or the heat. You can sense it and feel it, but you can't see it or touch it." J. D. was selling this girl something he hadn't thought much about himself in the last twenty years. He felt like a preacher and wondered if perhaps he was preaching as much to himself as to her.

"Well, maybe," Lizzie conceded, "but that still don't explain heaven. I ain't seen it, so I don't believe it. It's just that simple."

"Lizzie, you ever travel much?"

"I been to Raleigh."

"Have you ever been to California?"

"Heavens, no! That's a long way off."

"Do you believe there *is* a California?"

"Sure. It's in my geography book."

"You've never seen it, but you believe it's there. Just because a book tells you it is."

"Yeah, I reckon."

"It's the same thing, honey. It's the same thing. It's called faith."

J. D. felt for a moment as if he were talking to his own daughter. She looked so vulnerable and breakable and innocent. She could easily have been Angela's little sister. He wanted to protect her and teach her and help her with so many things she was going to face on her own. He thought of her father, a caring man, certainly, but cold and distant. J. D. couldn't imagine Paul talking to a young girl about the things she needed to know, the things any daughter needed to learn. Her mother was gone. As J. D. sat there, he felt emotionally sick at Lizzie's chances. Life, if she lived, would not be easy. He had no idea of her education—how far along in school she was. She seemed bright, but …

A voice came from the shadows behind him. "You about through here?"

It was Paul. J. D. stood and walked toward the doorway leading to the kitchen. He said to Lizzie, "I'll be back before I leave."

Paul Clem walked to the kitchen stove and took a sip of water from a tin dipper. He watched J. D. with eyes that trusted nothing.

"You're right, Mr. Clem. She's a sick girl. Are you willing now to move her to a hospital?"

"No."

"Can I bring a doctor?"

"No."

As Paul Clem dipped more water, he never took his eyes off J. D., and his face never changed expressions. He pointed casually with the dipper toward the table where he had set out all the groceries and said, "Where'd you get that milk?"

"Grocery store."

"I never seen milk put up like that."

J. D.'s pulse raced, and he felt perspiration at his temples. He knew he had to be careful in how he answered. What if he leveled with this man and told him what he knew? At worst, there might be an altercation and a little embarrassment. Or maybe this tired, life-beaten man, a product of the Depression, could shine some light on what was happening in both their lives. But he knew in his heart that Paul wasn't ready for that. No matter how much J. D. wanted to say something, he knew he wasn't going to confide in Paul Clem.

"That's called a, uh ... a carton. It's how ... uh ... some milk comes now."

J. D. ran the list of groceries quickly through his mind, trying to think what else he might have overlooked that would be a dead giveaway.

"Never seen nothin' but bottles."

"Really?" J. D. tried to sound casual. "This is something fairly … new."

"Everything you got is new, ain't it, boy? That automobile out there you're drivin.' Never seen nothin' like that around here before you showed up. Just everything about you. The clothes you wear; your haircut. And these strange paper sacks?" Paul held up one of the plastic bags tentatively between his fingers. "You're a slick one, ain't you?"

It was as if Paul Clem wanted to pick a fight. And maybe he did. This man had a lot of steam built up in him, and J. D. was becoming more and more aware that Paul was sensing something was amiss about the whole situation. But if he was ever going to be able to see Lizzie again, he had to defuse whatever was boiling in Paul Clem's mind.

"Mr. Clem, I'm going to want to come back in a day or two and check on Lizzie. I'll bring you anything you need when I come."

Paul Clem thought for a few seconds and said, "I could use a few things. A new hoe handle, some chicken feed and tobacco. And bring Lizzie somethin' to read. She likes books, and she may not get to school for a while this year."

"What year is she in at school?"

"High school. She's got a couple more years."

"I'll bring all that the next time I come. I guess I'd better be going, but I want to say good-bye to her before I go."

Paul nodded as permission, and J. D. walked back into the parlor. But he got only halfway across the room before he saw that the young girl was asleep. He walked quietly to the side of the bed. She had covered herself with blankets clear to her chin in this stifling hot room. Only her left hand was out from under the covers, and he could see she was clutching something in her fist. It was the bottle of pills he had left on the night table. He reached up and turned off the lamp and said a silent prayer for her health, her well-being, and the life journey ahead of her.

He walked back through the kitchen and stopped to say something, but Paul was nowhere to be found. When he stepped outside, he looked in all directions and even called Paul's name twice, but there was no answer. J. D. got in the van and started the engine, and just as he was about to back down the lane toward the road, he thought he saw someone at an upstairs window. He hit the brakes and looked again, but whoever or whatever it was, was gone. He sat for a moment and decided it was only a shadow or his eyes playing tricks on him. He put the van in reverse and backed out onto Route 814.

Chapter Nineteen

The downtown Dining Club was in the middle of the afternoon shift change. Karlie was sitting in the back corner booth working on an ad for the next day's newspaper. She was holding a ruler tight on her paper and printing her perfectly formed letters above it when she sensed someone standing at the table. She finished the line she was working on before looking up. It was Lottie, her purse in her hand and her blue sweater around her shoulders, preppy style.

"May I sit down, or are you busy?"

"The answer to both those questions is yes. I'd like the break."

Lottie looked serious but not nervous or concerned or even uneasy.

"Do we need to talk about what went on here yesterday?"

"Only if you feel a need to, Lottie."

"I guess I do." She forced a little laugh. "I wouldn't have come over to talk if I didn't think it was necessary. Would I be out of line to ask what happened with Crystal after I left yesterday?"

"Have you asked Crystal?"

"No. She didn't bring it up, so neither did I. I didn't want to embarrass anybody, and then I came in this morning and Katherine wasn't here. I'm just rather confused over everything."

"I'll be the first to admit things are sort of a mess right now, but I don't feel comfortable talking to you about the other girls. I think you can appreciate that."

"Oh, I do. Don't misunderstand. I'm just in the dark, and Randy was pretty upset when I told him about it last night. We just wanted to know where I stood. I guess Crystal is in the clear, and with Katherine gone, does that mean she's the guilty party? That's all we were wondering."

"Well, if Katherine's gone, it's of her own volition. I can't really answer that right now." Karlie watched Lottie fold a paper napkin into smaller and smaller squares. "And speaking of Randy—how's he doing?"

"Oh, he's fine. Things are going a lot better for us."

"Is he still working two jobs?"

As if a flash of yellow cartoon lightning had crackled across the table between them, Lottie pulled back, leaving the multifolded napkin on the table. She dropped her hands into her lap and pressed her lips together so tightly she had to spit her words out.

"Just what are you implying? If I say he's working just one job, would you suddenly think I'm the one who took the money? Is that what you're saying?"

"No," Karlie said calmly, "I'm not implying anything. I was simply asking if he was still working two jobs. Anything more you read into that is your own doing, Lottie."

"He quit his part-time job because he got a raise at Gillman Design. Is that what you wanted to hear?"

"Sounds like good news to me. Congratulations."

"I don't know what I expected to gain by talking to you. I just … well, I just always liked you so much, and I thought we could talk this thing out. But I have to be honest with you. I don't feel good about this. I think you have bad thoughts about me."

"Lottie, this is not an easy time for me. I'm handling this and a few other things that are precious to me right now with as much care and dignity as I can muster. I don't need you going off the deep end just because you want me to say something I'm not prepared to say. We have a problem here at the restaurant. It *will* be taken care of, and when it is, you'll know all about it in good time."

"Well, I guess there's nothing more to say on the matter. I'll be in tomorrow at the regular time unless I hear different from you or J. D. If you want me to quit you just let me know."

"We'll see you in the morning, Lottie. Have a nice evening."

$$\rightarrow$$

J. D. drove back to Hanson with mixed emotions running through his head. He knew he should call and cancel the four-fifteen appointment with Dr. Carnham, but he couldn't bring himself to care about that right now. He was glad to have gotten the penicillin to Lizzie, and yet he couldn't be sure that would solve all her problems. He didn't feel good about Paul and how they had left things. If he went back—no, make that *when* he went back—he didn't know if Paul would open the door to him again. And when should he go back? Tonight? Tomorrow? The next day? It was the same calendar date now, but what would it be the next time? The same year? A different month? Two weeks later? He couldn't find a single minute of peace about any of this. And what would he say to Karlie? He knew that as soon as he told her, she would make him promise never to go again. He didn't want to put himself in that situation. This couldn't go on forever. Or what if it did? What if it went on until the times collided? No. He had to get those thoughts out of his head. They only made the back of his neck and the top of his skull ache. He had to clear his head a little before he got home. But first, he had one important stop to make.

His knock was answered swiftly and with a smile.

"J. D. Wickman, come in, come in."

"I hope you don't mind me dropping in like this, Ms. Justice, but I thought I needed to see you."

"Not at all. I'm glad you did. How did things go with Navin?"

"Navin? Ah, you mean Dr. Annata. Just perfect. He gave me exactly what I wanted, and I was out of there in minutes."

"He's a good man. A little unconventional, but a good man. Have a seat."

J. D. sat down in the same blue wing-backed chair he had sat in two days before. Lavern Justice sat on the end of the sofa closest to him. She waited for him to speak, and he could see she was anxious for him to begin. She was like a child waiting to be told a secret.

"First, thank you for your help today. I couldn't have pulled any of this off without you. Not legally anyway."

Lavern laughed, "I'm not sure how legal it was, but I'm glad it worked. Did it work?"

"I think so. I saw the girl and gave her the amoxicillin and left her with the instructions. Keep your fingers crossed."

"Good. What else? There's some other reason you're here."

"Yes, there is. I need more help from you. I need to find out who this family is, and I know you can do it in half the time it would take me. You worked in the courthouse, and you know how to trace someone and do research on them. I don't. So will you help me?"

"Of course I will, J. D. Let me get a pen and paper."

She reached over to a drawer under her coffee table and took out a tablet and a number two pencil. She wrote something at the top of the page and then looked up at J. D. "Fire away."

"This girl's name is Lizzie Clem. She's sixteen years old, and it's 1942—so that means she was born in 1926, depending on exactly when her birthday is. I don't know that. Her father is Paul Clem, and her mother was Ada. If she's alive today she'd be … what, eighty-one years old? Chances are she's not living today. I have no idea. But either way, there has to be a birth certificate or something on her. I just want some sort of proof that there was or is such a person as Lizzie Clem. Do you have any idea how to go about researching all that?"

Lavern finished writing before she looked up. When she did, she rubbed her chin with her index finger and said, "Tomorrow is Friday. I can start on the Internet this evening and then go to the courthouse in the morning. I'll call you by at least Monday noon. Maybe before."

"You don't mind doing this, do you, Lavern?" He called her by her first name before even thinking.

"Are you kidding me, young man? You give an old woman reason to live!"

$$\rightarrow$$

Karlie was putting a casserole in the oven, and Angela, who was supposed to be making the salad, was sitting at the kitchen island eating lettuce from the bowl. Angela watched her mother a long time before she drummed up the courage to say what was nearly bursting her head open. She didn't want to invade on an old family secret, but at the same time she felt she deserved to know the truth. This time alone with her mother was as good a time as any. Just getting the first word out was the trick. Once the commitment was made with that first word, the conversation would take care of itself.

"Mamma, can I ask you something?"

"Sure, honey. Here, take this pitcher and fill it with ice cubes. What do you want to ask me?"

Angela stood at the refrigerator and dipped ice cubes into the glass tea pitcher, straining to think of the right words. She didn't want to embarrass her mother. But, at the same time, she desperately wanted to let her know that she was aware of a truth that her mother had never bothered to share.

"Didn't you and Daddy graduate from college together?"

"Yes, we did. May 24, 1986. We set our wedding date that same night and got married three months later."

"You even remember the date of graduation?"

"You will too, honey. So many dates that are important in your life just seem to stick with you. Why do you ask?"

"I was just wondering." Angela was back at the salad bowl eating snips of lettuce. "But didn't you and Daddy go to high school together also?"

"Sure did. *We'll give it a try—do it or die—at Hanson High.* Your daddy lettered in baseball, and I was a cheerleader—and, of course, baseball is the one sport that doesn't have cheerleaders. So I was traveling all over the state with the football team and the basketball team, and then when baseball season came around I couldn't go to all the games unless I got a ride with someone. I caused a big stir his senior year."

"What happened?"

"I went to the athletic director, Mr. Scone. And don't think we didn't have fun with that name. Anyway, I complained to him that baseball didn't have cheerleaders and I didn't think it was fair to the team in the name of school spirit and all that stuff. Well, surprisingly, he agreed with me and urged me to register a complaint—those were his words, 'register a complaint'—with the principal and the school board."

"No, you didn't!" And Angela began to laugh.

"Oh, I'm afraid I did. I made quite the scene. Put up posters all over school."

"What did they say?"

"The posters, or the school board?" And Karlie was laughing too.

"Both," Angela said through her giggles.

"The posters said something like 'Baseball is a school sport too' and ... oh dear, I don't remember anymore. But the school board—I went to one of their meetings and they let me state my case, and then they discussed it. It was in the papers, and what a mess! Your granddaddy Bill finally said, 'Enough,' and it just sort of died away, but I had a lot of fun with it at the time."

"This was your senior year?" Angela asked.

"That was my junior year. Your father's senior year."

"So you two didn't graduate from high school together?"

"No. He was a year ahead of me."

Angela took a deep breath and remembered everything her grandmother had recently told her. How he had wanted to quit and wait for his girlfriend so they could go off to college together. And how he had not been the perfect student that first year.

"If he was a year ahead of you in high school, how did it work out that you both graduated from college together?" Angela stared into the lettuce bowl, almost afraid to catch her mother's eye. She was pretty certain they'd kept her father's decision to leave school that first month a secret because it paralleled her own situation much too closely. She didn't look up for fear of seeing the look on her mother's face that surely told the whole story. But her mother's answer and the tone of her voice gave nothing of the sort away.

"I finished in four years, and your father took five. He worked part time all the way through school, so he took a lighter schedule than I did. He worked for an electrician that did mostly campus maintenance, and I used to tease him that he spent more time in the girls' dorm than he did in the guys'. He was crawling around in every closet and attic and cubbyhole in the basements."

Karlie stopped what she was doing and looked directly and curiously at her daughter and said, "Why do you ask?"

"Just wondered," Angela said and tried to appear off-handed.

"If you'll set the table, we'll eat in about fifteen minutes. That is, if your daddy is home, and he should be by then."

"Mamma, do you think, after we eat dinner, that it would be too late for me to go see Grandma again?"

"Not at all. She stays up late like you wouldn't believe. She's always telling me who's on Leno. I'm sure she'd love to see you."

Chapter Twenty

Friday morning found the three Wickmans where they usually were at 7:00 a.m. Karlie was in the kitchen, dressed and making coffee; Angela was in her room, surely still asleep; and J. D. was standing in his bathroom with only his shoes and pants on, shaving. Last night had been a good and relaxing evening. After dinner, Angela had gone to Maple Manor to visit J. D.'s mother, and before going to close up the restaurants, he and Karlie had cleaned up the kitchen and talked more than they had in weeks. She told him about her early-morning visit from Katherine and then her later conversation with Lottie. They analyzed together what all of that meant and came up short of anything concrete. Later, they all watched a Woody Allen movie on cable, ate ice cream, and went to bed.

It had been as close to a normal night as he had spent in the past four days. And it would have been perfect if he could have shared with Karlie what had happened at the Clem house, but he knew that would only open up avenues he didn't want to go down. He had finally decided it was best to enjoy the family moment and keep the rest to himself. He wasn't used to doing that. He had never endured anything nearly as stressful as this without either Karlie or Jack. And it looked like neither one of them was with him on this one. As he was realizing more with each passing day, he was alone. Except for … and he almost laughed aloud as he realized for the first time that his only confederate and friend in this was now Lavern Justice. A more unlikely pair never roamed the west or solved a mystery. And here they were. Wickman and Justice.

He saw Karlie's face appear in the mirror, and her expression made him turn quickly and say, "What's wrong?"

"You won't believe what I just found on the front porch."

"What?"

"I went out to get the paper, and this box was lying there next to it."

"What is it?"

The back doorbell rang, but she continued with another thought. "That'll be Caywood. I called him just now before I ran up here. He was on his way to work. He was only a couple of blocks away. Come on down while I let him in, and I'll show you both at the same time."

Caywood? J. D. thought. What was going on? What did she find that would cause her to call the police before she even told *him* about it? He tossed the electric razor back on its shelf and grabbed a shirt as he ran out the door and down the steps. When he reached the bottom of the steps, Karlie was just letting Bobby Caywood in the back door.

"Good morning, Bobby, and thank you for coming," Karlie greeted him.

"You sounded scared. Morning, J. D. What's up?"

Karlie looked from Bobby to J. D. "I went out to get the paper off the porch just a few minutes ago and saw this box there beside it. I picked it up and opened it, thinking it was some sort of advertisement or maybe something from the paper man. I took the top off it and ..."

She took the top off the little box and held it out for Bobby and J. D. to see simultaneously. Bobby was the first to reach for it. He pulled the wad of money out of the box, held it up, looked at J. D. and Karlie and said, "How much is here?"

"I don't know," Karlie said. "I haven't had a chance to count it. Is it okay to touch it?"

"Yeah," Caywood assured her. "You can't get prints off money—there's thousands on there. Now the box is a different story. You may have messed up some on the box. Or maybe not."

J. D. reached for the money, sat down at the kitchen counter, and began counting. Caywood and Karlie said nothing until he was finished.

"One thousand thirty," he said, setting it on the countertop.

"How much?" Caywood asked.

"One thousand thirty dollars."

"That's an odd amount. Does that number mean anything to either one of you?"

Karlie shook her head and said, "No."

J. D. checked inside the box for a note or some other clue and said, "Maybe."

Bobby Caywood waited a few seconds, then impatiently said, "Okay, are you going to tell me, or do you want me to start guessing?"

"No, I was just trying to figure. You asked me the other day how much money had been stolen from the restaurant, and I was trying to remember what I said."

"I can tell you exactly what you said." And Caywood reached in his coat pocket and pulled out a small tablet. He leafed through it and said, "Monday, September tenth—two thirty—I asked you how much was missing. Karlie said less than a thousand dollars. J. D. said nine hundred seventy-eight dollars and change." He looked at J. D. "You seemed pretty sure."

"Well, you know how that goes. If it were expenditures or income I would be sure. But when someone's stealing from you, dollars can fall through the cracks. I could have been off some. How much difference is that? Difference between one thousand thirty to nine hundred seventy-eight. That's only fifty-two dollars. I could easily have been off fifty-two dollars. It was only my best estimate at the time."

Bobby Caywood looked at both of them. "Where does all this stand since we left it at the restaurant Wednesday? Any confessions you two haven't told me about? Any changes of habit?"

"Yes and no," Karlie interjected. "Katherine came back here to talk to me, and we had some uncomfortable words. She was hurt— but as far as a confession, no. Although she hasn't been back to work since, unless she's there this morning. And then Lottie and I talked yesterday. It was the same sort of conversation. She was upset because she had been suspected and wanted to know where she stood. But no one has come out and showed their hand."

"Crystal?" Caywood asked. "Has she said anything more?"

"Nothing. You heard everything she had to say the other day."

The three of them sat in silence. Caywood was the first to speak. "I'll take the box with me and have it dusted, but I don't think you'll find anything. It's too easy to wear gloves. And if I had to say, I would bet this is the last you will ever hear of it. This is most likely the exact amount stolen, even if you can't verify it. And my twenty years of experience tells me you will never know for sure who left it here this morning. And knowing you two, you probably don't want to."

"I really didn't want it to end this way," J. D. said. "I know Karlie can accept this better than I can, but I've always liked things tied up and ended. 'Course, I'm learning more every day that's not always the case, but it doesn't keep me from wishing it was."

"Well, get over that, buddy. This is life. Not *Perry Mason* or *Law and Order*. You don't always get the bad guy in the end. Sometimes he gets you. But if you had to make the choice of getting the money back or knowing who took it, wouldn't you rather have the money back?"

Caywood continued as he folded his pad and put it back in his inside coat pocket. "Everything that happens in life isn't always tied up with a pretty bow on it. There will always be loose ends that keep us up at night. Facts that don't add up. But you know what? You don't grieve over the ones you can't solve. Take the best from it. Give the woman, whichever one she may be, the benefit of the doubt and keep a closer eye on things in the future. But don't fret over it. And don't be too hard on yourself for not demanding an absolute and flawless answer. God knows there just isn't always one to have."

Bobby opened the back door to leave, and Karlie said, "Thank you so much for coming by. We really appreciate all you've done."

"That's okay. You owe me a free lunch, and we'll be even."

"Owe you one?" J. D. said. "When was the last time you paid for one?"

Caywood smiled and said to Karlie as he was closing the door, "Tell your husband I said good-bye."

Karlie stood in the middle of the kitchen floor with her arms folded, looking at the stack of money, while J. D. sat on the high-back stool, elbows on the counter, and rubbed the smooth side of his face.

"What do we do now?" she asked.

"I am so tired with everything that's going on. You know what? How about we do nothing. If this is how it's meant to be, let's close the book on it."

"Can you do that?"

"Probably not, but I'm willing to try if you are. I'm trading in my pretty bows for loose ends. Save me some of that coffee while I go shave the other side of my face."

$\rightarrow$

Eight o'clock found Karlie through with her makeup and J. D. finished with his shaving and dressing and the both of them at the kitchen table eating breakfast. J. D. had made a call to the down-town restaurant and was only mildly surprised to hear Katherine answer the phone. He told her to call him when the produce truck came later in the day since he wanted to be there when they unloaded. She seemed her old, natural self and said good-bye as cheerily as she said hello. Karlie asked if Lottie and Crystal were in, and J. D. replied that he hadn't asked but was sure that if they hadn't been, Katherine would have said so. The TV was tuned to *The Today Show,* J. D was checking the high school football sched-ule in the morning paper, and Karlie was reading the news on her laptop, which was sitting next to her toast and coffee. The seren-ity of the scene was at once added to and then disrupted by their daughter's entrance.

"Good morning," she said with a song in her voice.

Karlie and J. D. turned at the same time, shared looks of surprise on their faces. But as surprised as they were at her being dressed and downstairs at 8:00 a.m., they were even more shocked at what she was setting on the floor.

"Is that your suitcase?" her mother asked.

"It's actually an old one of yours. It's a little bigger than mine, and I wanted to take some more winter clothes with me."

"Where exactly are you going?" her father asked.

"Back to school. Don't you remember, Daddy, that I told you there was a mixer there this weekend I wanted to go to?"

"Yeah, I remember, but then you said you didn't really want to go...."

She laughed. "Of course I want to go! They're going to have a live band and everything. And maybe I need to try a little harder or at least give it a little more time. I put that dress in here, Mamma, the one we bought last spring when we went over to Dillard's in Charlotte. You know the pink one with that swoop neck?"

"Angela," Karlie began, her tone more concerned than bewildered, "are you going back to school, or are you just going back to this dance? And then pop in here again next week with the same story? If you are, I think we had better have …"

"Oh, Mamma, don't be silly. I'm going back to school. That's what you want me to do, isn't it? I mean isn't that what you both want me to do?"

"Yes, that's what we want you to do," said Karlie. "And I hope that's what you want to do. But if this is not settled in your mind, I think now is a good time to settle it. You need to make a commitment and stick to it. You're either in school or you're not. Can you keep your commitment?"

"Yes. I know I can. Tell her, Daddy. I know if I go back that's it. And I'll see you at Thanksgiving or maybe once before depending on if I can get a ride."

"Speaking of a ride," said J. D., "how are you traveling this morning?"

"Jenna is picking me up. She comes home a lot of the time during the week. She has a weird schedule. I called her last night."

"You decided last night you were going back to school?"

"Yeah. Pretty much."

"Sweetheart, I don't want to say anything that might make you change your mind, but I have to risk it. When did all this change? And why? Less than forty-eight hours ago you were standing right here on this very spot, adamantly telling us you weren't going back to school until January. Now you have your bags packed. Excuse me—your mother's bags packed. What happened?"

"Do you really want me to tell you?"

"Certainly I do. I'm a little baffled. Happy but baffled."

"Grandma changed my mind." Angela sat down at the table between her parents and spoke to them like the adult she was bound to become. "She told me some things I didn't know. She's always full of surprises, but this time she told me about her feelings when she went to college. And how she and Granddaddy both had that nervous, uneasy feeling in their stomachs being away from home for the first time. That everybody has that feeling, and that it's not just me. And, Daddy, she told me about you coming home on Thanksgiving break that first year and telling the whole family you were quitting school for a whole year. And she told me why." The tears started in her voice and then welled up in her blue eyes. "She told me you wanted to wait on Mamma so you could go all through college together. Oh, Mamma, I think that's the sweetest thing I've ever heard in my entire life, and I don't hold it against you for not telling me the whole truth last night."

She leaned over and hugged her mother so tightly she nearly lost her balance. As J. D. was reaching for her arm to keep her from falling, a car horn blasted three times from the driveway.

"That will be Jenna. I love you guys."

"Call us when you get there," Karlie ordered.

"I will. Bye, Daddy. Tell Grandma I love her. I told her last night, but tell her again for me."

They kissed her good-bye and, their offer of help refused, watched her sling the family suitcase into Jenna's trunk, then watched the car back out into the street. They closed the door slowly but didn't return to their seats at the table. They stood looking at each other.

"Did your mother and dad go to college?" Karlie asked.

"Not that I know of. Dad might have gone to some night school after work at one time, but I'm pretty sure Mom never set foot on a campus. And what's all this about me wanting to quit school so we could graduate together?"

"Something Miss Beatrice put in her head. I have no idea."

"Well, it worked. While everything we were saying was falling short of even reaching her ears, Miss Beatrice's words worked magic."

They laughed, and Karlie said, "That's your mother. I wonder what other stories she makes up and tells about you and me to those sweet old ladies over there."

Chapter Twenty-one

After a morning like that, J. D. didn't need any more excitement to make this day memorable. He was hoping it might take on some degree of normalcy, yet he was anxiously awaiting a call from Lavern Justice that could make everything that had already happened today pale in comparison. But by noon that call hadn't come. He walked up the street to the Coffee Cup and had just what the name suggested with Rollie Doyle, his nearest competitor. They were joined by a couple of other merchant friends, and he enjoyed the diversion of small talk. They agreed to have their monthly poker game the following week, and he issued the invitation to hold it in his basement. It would be one of those friendly little games with no more than twenty bucks at stake. J. D. didn't really think of it as gambling. It was just good, cheap fun. A night out at the movies could cost Karlie and him a lot more than he could lose in one poker sitting. The ticket price for two plus popcorn and Cokes would be closer to twenty-five dollars, and they always ran the chance of seeing a bad movie. At least with poker night, he always knew what to expect, and it was fun—win, lose, or draw.

By two o'clock he still had heard nothing from Lavern, and he knew it would be futile to call. She would let him know as soon as she had any useful information. He made up his mind that if he hadn't heard anything by four, he would chance another trip to the bridge and see if Lizzie was feeling any improvement from the medicine. In the meantime, he needed to pick up the items Paul Clem had told him he wanted. A hoe handle, some chicken feed, and tobacco. "And bring Lizzie somethin' to read." He could find something for her at Valley News down the block. They had every magazine and paperback known to man. He popped in there on his way back to the restaurant and began searching through the shelves and stacks.

He quickly realized any magazine was out of the question. They were all filled with current news. The covers were full of Justin Timberlake and Britney Spears and *American Idol*. She would be expecting a magazine like *Life* or *Look* and stories on Gary Cooper and Joan Crawford. He walked to the bookshelves. John Grisham, Stephen King, and Mary Higgins Clark kept looking back at him. This was no good. He couldn't take today's books to her. On the back shelf, he found what he was looking for: a stack of used paperbacks. Some were in pretty bad shape, but at least they would have the right date in them. He ran his finger across the titles and noticed two Nancy Drew novels. *The Mystery of the Brass-Bound Trunk,* copyrighted 1940. Perfect. And another one, *The Quest of the Missing Map,* dated 1942. One more. He wasn't sure what reading level she was and if these would be too young for her or hit just right. So to balance it out he decided on Agatha Christie, *The Body in the Library,* 1942. She would probably never notice the dates, but if she did, he was covered. He didn't want to offer up any more suspicion than was necessary.

He thought about the items Paul wanted and where he might find them. The tobacco wouldn't be hard to find. He could find the hoe handle at a hardware store. But the chicken feed could be a little tricky. Then he remembered the Barn and Farm Store out on Clancy Pike. He hadn't been there in years, but it was only a ten-minute drive and would probably be worth the trouble.

The parking lot was full of pickup trucks, cattle trucks, and family sedans. The Barn and Farm Store was huge and had everything from groceries to hardware to bib overalls and work boots to chicken and cattle feed. He parked and went inside and was immediately met with a strange odor suggesting a mixture of grain, floor polish, and flannel. The store was permeated from front to back with this not unpleasant but very peculiar smell. He looked around for a clerk to help him and spotted a large red-faced man with a name tag on his pocket informing the world his name was Leonard. Leonard's neck was too large for his shirt and his legs were too short for his pants, and his attitude was favorable only toward those who knew what they were looking for. He was leaning on a bin full of half-priced house paint. He had a toothpick in one side of his mouth and looked like he didn't want to be disturbed.

"Do you work here?" J. D. asked.

"Most of the day. What can I do for you?"

"I'm looking for a hoe handle."

"A hoe handle! Just a handle?"

"Yeah, I think so."

"There's some back here, but why would you want just a handle? It'll cost you as much as a new hoe."

He walked ahead of J. D. through a couple of aisles and stopped at a display that held wooden shovel and hoe and rake handles.

"We don't sell many of these anymore. I don't know why anybody would want to buy one. You'd have to know how to put one on, and you don't look like you do."

"Well, actually you're right. It's not for me. I was just getting what someone told me he needed."

"Well, you don't need this. Get a new hoe. They only cost about two dollars more than the handle. Here." He handed J. D. a new hoe from a neighboring rack.

J. D. took the hoe without further comment or argument.

"Next I need some chicken feed."

Leonard actually squinted and sneered at him. "What kind?"

"What kind?" J. D. asked back. "Are you saying what brand?"

"No, I'm saying what kind. There's all kinds of chicken feed."

"I guess I just want regular chicken feed. I don't know much about that either."

"Obviously." Leonard snorted. And then he reeled off a list that was meant to put the city boy in his place. "You got Chick Starter, Pullet Builder, Egg Maker Pellets, Concentrate. And you can get it in bulk or get it in bags."

If he meant to stop J. D. cold, he had just succeeded. "Ah, maybe Pullet Builder. Is that pretty normal?"

"For a pullet it is. You got pullets?"

"I don't know."

"You're buying chicken feed, and you don't know what a pullet is?"

"Yeah, I guess I am, Leonard." J. D. was liking this man less and less all the time.

"A pullet is a layin' hen. You got layin' hens?"

"I think I've already told you I'm not buying this for myself."

"Well, I would hope not. I hope you're buying it for the chickens." And then he threw his head back and laughed way too big and too long at his own joke.

"Give me a hundred-pound bag of Pullet Builder."

"Don't come like that. It comes in fifty-pound bags."

"Then give me two bags. Now that's not so hard, is it?"

Leonard seemed to back off a little. "That's eight dollars and sixty cents a bag. What else you need?"

"Nothing."

Leonard wrote out a ticket, handed it to him, and said, "Pay at the register and drive around to the dock, and it'll be waitin' on you."

J. D. took the ticket and walked toward the checkout counter with the new hoe in his hand. He stopped at the tobacco case. He knew as little about tobacco as he did chicken feed, but he wasn't about to ask anyone else for help. Still, questions ran through his mind. Did Paul want chewing tobacco? Pipe tobacco? Cigarettes? Loose tobacco to roll himself? There was no way to be sure. He looked over all the brands and remembered some history trivia about the slogan "Lucky Strike Goes to War." His grandfather used to talk about it. But hadn't they changed the white on the package to Army green? That was no good. Then how about Camels? He knew that was an old brand and hadn't changed much. It still had a picture of a camel on it. Maybe Paul wouldn't notice the change in design or the taste, if there was any. He told the lady behind the counter he would take a carton of Camels. She came around with the key and opened the case, took one out, and handed it to him with the comment, "You know those things will kill you, don't you?"

"Naw, the chicken feed will get me first," he shot back.

"What?"

"Nothing. How much is all this?"

$\rightarrow$

Karlie was cleaning in the den and didn't hear the phone until she happened to turn off the vacuum cleaner. She ran to pick it up.

"Hello?"

"Karlie."

"Jack. Haven't talked to you in ages."

"I know. It's been a while."

"If you're looking for J. D., you can find him on his cell. He should be around someplace."

"Actually, I was looking for you. I knew he wouldn't be there in the middle of the day, and I wanted to talk to you."

"Okay," she said slowly, afraid and sure something was coming she didn't want to hear or talk about.

"This thing with J. D. and that bridge. What's going on with all that?"

"How much has he told you?"

"Everything, I guess. Told me you thought he was crazy and needed to see a doctor. He took me out there just like he did you."

"And what happened?"

"What do you think happened? Nothing. There's some kind of country convenience store out there. It's just a country road like a hundred others in the county. I'm calling, I guess, because I'm sort of worried. I don't mean to worry you, and I would never do anything to betray J. D. I'd fight, die, and lie for him. But this thing has got a hold of him, and I'm scared about it."

"I know, Jack. Me, too. He's had so much on him lately. His mother in the nursing home. Angela at school and then out of school and then back. The restaurants. I wish we had never taken on the second one. The headaches outweigh the income. You knew somebody was stealing from us at the downtown site, didn't you?"

"I heard. Did you get 'em?"

"We may never know who it was."

"What can I do? I'll do anything. You know that."

"Why don't you two take off and go to a ball game somewhere? Make a two- or three-day trip of it. Get him away. Get him thinking about something else besides … besides that. You know what I mean?"

"I can do that. If he'll go."

"He'll go if you insist. And the sooner the better."

"I'll call him tonight or tomorrow and plan something."

"Thanks, Jack. You're a good friend. By the way, how's the love life?"

"What's that? I'm not familiar with that word."

Karlie laughed. "Good-bye, Jack, and thanks for calling."

"Bye."

$$\rightarrow$$

Summer wasn't even beginning to act like it was over. J. D. was thankful for the patches of shade that appeared on the country roads and gave a nice respite to the early evening heat beating down on top of his head. He had driven the TR3 this morning and was glad he had because Paul had made some unsettling comments yesterday. He had accepted the sports car without much suspicion better than he had the van on the subsequent trips. The old guy was country and maybe hadn't darkened a lot of schoolhouse doors, but he was no fool. He had an instinct most educated people fail to nurture. J. D. had noticed that most erudite people were the most trusting, thinking everyone as upstanding as they were and consequently leaving their backs open for undue advantages. Not Paul Clem. He gave no one a break because no one had ever given him a break. His eyes told J. D. that he wasn't ever going to turn his back on him or believe half of what he was telling him. J. D. had to admit he was a little apprehensive about pulling up that lane again today just because of Paul Clem's attitude. He wasn't afraid of him, but he was constantly aware that the situation could become explosive.

His cell phone was ringing. He hated to talk on the phone with the top down. The wind whistling around his head made it almost impossible to hear clearly, but it might be Lavern. He reached for it and looked at the screen. Jack. He let it ring again and then again. He wasn't sure what they had to say to each other that was of much importance. He didn't want to blame Jack because he could certainly see how hard it must be for even an old friend to accept such an outlandish story. But what would it have hurt to give him a handful of penicillin tablets? It's not like somebody could get high off of them. They were to save someone's life, for heaven's sakes. Still, J. D. understood his friend's reluctance. He had to respect the fact that Jack was a professional, that he was serious about his career. It rang a fourth time. One more, and the voice mail would kick in.

"Hello."

"J. D. Where did I catch you? At work?"

"No. I'm on the road. What's going on?"

"Just checking in with you. Haven't heard from you in a couple of days."

"Yeah, I know. I've been busy."

"You been back out to that bridge?"

"I'm on my way there now. Why?"

"I just wondered. Has anything else happened?"

"Yeah, plenty's happened. I found a doctor who gave me some amoxicillin, and I took the pills to the girl. That was nearly twenty-seven hours ago. I'm on my way back out there to see if she's any better."

The pause at the other end was so long that J. D. thought he might have lost the connection, but he was determined he wouldn't be the first one to continue the conversation. Jack had called him. Let him say something if he wanted to.

"Are you telling me you actually saw these people again?" Jack finally asked.

"I'm telling you."

"J. D., I know you're not all that happy with me right now, and I wish I could do or say something to make it up to you...."

"You can."

"Really? What?"

"Give me some medical info. It's been nearly twenty-seven hours since I was out here. The first pill was at two yesterday. Then another at eight last night. Then one at two a.m. Then one at eight this morning and another at two this afternoon. That means she has taken five pills total. Is that enough to start to show some improvement?"

"Oh, yeah. It should be in her system good by five doses. But don't count on five."

"Why not?"

"Well, when doctors say every six hours, people are always confused if that means literally every six hours or just when you're up and awake. Most people don't get up at two a.m. to take a pill. They should, but they don't."

"I think she would. And I'm hoping she did."

For those few seconds the banter between the old friends seemed natural and unstrained. Then Jack asked, "Who was the doctor that gave you the prescription?"

"You don't really want to know that, do you?"

"No, I guess not. Hey, anyway, the reason I was calling. You want to go catch a Panthers game this weekend? I can get some tickets, and I know a girl in Charlotte—you know, the one I told you about—who can get us a last-minute hotel room with no problem."

"No, I don't think so."

"Why not? Come on. It'll be fun to get away. You're not scared Karlie won't let you go, are you?"

J. D. laughed. "No. Truth be known, she's probably the one who put you up to asking me. Maybe some other time."

The pause this time was longer than the last. J. D. waited just long enough to know in his heart he had hit the nail on the head and then finally said, "Gotta go. Talk to you later." And snapped his phone shut.

Just as he did, the hoe sticking out of the car shifted. He grabbed it to make sure it wouldn't jump out on a sharp turn. The hundred pounds of chicken feed was packed in the small trunk so tightly that there was no chance of it shifting anywhere. He was less than a mile from the bridge, and his only thought was how relieved he would be if Lizzie met him at the door. That would prove in short order that she was on the mend. He had decided to stay a little longer this time and talk to Paul. He really wanted to win him over and make him comfortable with the situation. He was so preoccupied with these thoughts that it never crossed his mind that the one lane bridge might not be there when he rounded the final curve. But it wasn't.

Only Stan's One Stop.

$$\rightarrow$$

What had happened? He never considered he might not be able to cross any time he wished. He was sure he had figured out everything that could possibly be of importance. The vehicles, the time of day, the passengers. What else could it be? There was only one other possibility. His Mission. Was the Mission over?

As he drove back into town with the wind blowing in his face, clouds boiled up behind him and settled deep into a dark gray sky. It looked like it would surely rain before he got home. And he didn't care. He hoped it would.

Chapter Twenty two

That night, Friday night, was one of the longest and most miserable nights of his life. He couldn't eat. He couldn't sleep. And every time he looked at Karlie, he was reminded that she and Jack had plotted against him. When did they talk? What did they say? They were certainly on the same page about this whole Route 814 matter. Maybe they were also plotting to have him committed. And he was only half joking about that prospect.

He didn't feel like talking, so he spent most of his evening in the basement. Since he still hadn't heard anything from Lavern, he got on his computer for about an hour and tried to look up birth certificate information himself. This turned out to be in vain. He kept running into obstacles—forms to fill out or disclaimers that told him that that kind of personal information could only be given to family members who could prove their kinship. He was sure Lavern had the experience to get around those obstacles, or at least he was hoping she could. Maybe he was putting too much stock in *her*. Maybe she was just a nice little lady with a high curiosity threshold who was leading him on for her own personal adventure. Maybe she was reporting everything they had talked about to Karlie and Jack. Maybe she and her Dr. Annata were the ones who would finally have him strapped and straitjacketed and hauled to the nearest loony bin in town. Or maybe he was just growing more paranoid with each passing minute.

In all honesty, he felt Lavern Justice was on the level. But he had to pinch himself occasionally to wake himself up and remind his tired, weary alter ego that she was the only friend he had where all of this was concerned. Here was a woman just a few years short of twice his age whom he had only known for three days—and she was the only person he could depend on. The only one who would help him. How had he gotten himself into this quagmire that had practically destroyed all avenues of communication between him and his wife and his best friend? He wanted out of the mess, but he had no idea how to achieve that. He also wanted to see the Clems again to be assured all was well by the bridge. He didn't know how to do that either.

He spent the best part of the night on the patio, looking at the stars and dozing. It wasn't until 2:00 a.m., time for Lizzie's pill, that he got up and went to bed. He was sure Karlie heard him, but she never said a word.

→

Saturday morning in the Wickman household was pretty much like any weekday morning. Karlie and J. D. got up at the same time and usually went to different restaurants around nine. This Saturday Karlie was going downtown, and he was going to the west end. All this had been planned earlier in the week. Little else was discussed over the breakfast table. As she was clearing the table she did finally say, "Have you talked to Jack lately?"

That was all he needed to confirm what he already knew. But he held his tongue and his temper. Even though he felt betrayed and angry, he knew in his heart Jack and Karlie were doing it for love.

"He called me yesterday."

"And?"

"And he told me you two had talked and decided I should take a trip with him for a couple of days to a football game, and that maybe then I would come to my senses and forget all about this crazy idea of those people out on Route 814." J. D. spoke plainly, but the words had a bite to them that didn't require an angry tone.

As hard as Karlie tossed the plates into the sink, it was a wonder they didn't shatter. "J. D., what makes you strike out at me like that? If Jack told you that, and I don't think he did, it was a good idea either way. Why *don't* you leave for a couple of days? You sure aren't happy here."

"If I do, it won't be with Jack. I'll be by myself." This time, he spoke sharply. And he left the table and went upstairs to finish dressing. When he came back down, she had gone.

Just as he was putting on his sport coat and opening the back door, the phone rang. He looked at the caller ID before answering, sure that it was Karlie. It was a number he didn't recognize. He picked it up after the second ring.

"Hello."

"J. D.? This is Lavern Justice."

"I've been waiting on your call. How did things go?"

"I think we should talk. Where's a good place, and what's a good time?"

"How about the same restaurant at ten? I'll have the coffee hot and the booth empty."

"Sounds good. But make mine decaf this time. That real stuff gives me palpitations. And you make it strong!"

"Made to order, Ms. Justice. See you at ten."

His mood brightened. Maybe he was about to get some information that would answer lingering questions about who Lizzie Clem was and why she was popping up in his life. And if she was real. And if she was alive. And all the other *ifs* that had kept him awake for the past week. His mind was tired, but he felt he was on the verge of relief.

$$\rightarrow$$

J. D. was sitting in the booth, reading the Saturday morning paper, two empty cups in front of him, when the door opened at precisely 10:00 a.m. and the small and erect Lavern came through it with a breeze. She walked briskly to the booth and slid in as he stood to greet her.

"Sit down. Sit down. You don't have to stand up for me."

She appeared drawn, and with her hair pulled tightly back from her face she looked her age for the first time. She was smiling, but only with her mouth—the smile never reached her eyes. As he sat back down, she sighed heavily and reached for the empty cup. "There's nothing in here."

"It's coming," he assured her. He didn't want to ask her if she had been up all night researching and allude to the fact that she looked less than perky and alert. So he ignored that line of conversation altogether and simply said, "How are you this morning?"

"Alive, grouchy, and mean as ever."

"I hope you have good news … although I'll admit I'm not sure what I'm expecting."

"I have news, but I'm not sure if it's good. Let me tell you a little about public records. They are reliable *if* you can find them. They aren't always easy to locate. This Elizabeth Clem, and I'm only assuming her name is Elizabeth, is a tough nut."

"I can't be sure. Lizzie is all I know."

"Birth certificate laws vary from state to state. There were no federal standards in the early twentieth century when Elizabeth was born. I went online first, but to be honest, J. D.—and you probably know this—you can't always depend on the records you find online for anything. But the NCHS had certain records for live births back then."

"Wait a minute. What's NCHS?"

"National Center for Health Statistics. That was and is the official standard, but only if the individual states complied. In reality, it took a while for all the states to get in line with their registration. The northeastern states were the first, and it wasn't until the 1930s that it got real strict. And we're talking about a birth that took place in rural North Carolina in 1926."

"So the bottom line is …"

"The bottom line is, we could have missed it by four, five, six, seven years."

"Did you check all the courthouses in the state?"

"As well as I could. I checked state records and all the surrounding county records. Today you have a record of every birth, every marriage, every death. Marriage and death records are more accurate and more likely to be recorded. As you can imagine, you could have had a birth back in those days on a farm thirty miles from nowhere without even a doctor in attendance. Ah, here's the girl with my coffee. But you know, honey, I've changed my mind. I don't think I want any right now."

The conversation came to a complete halt while Marge filled just J. D.'s cup and set the pot on the table. As soon as she left, Lavern Justice continued.

"The record of choice in those days and the years earlier was the family Bible. A page from the family Bible is just as binding and legal as a registered birth certificate. Unfortunately, we don't have that either. You don't have her family Bible, do you?"

"No. I don't even know if there was one."

"Can you get one? There might be one in the house."

J. D. didn't want to tell her that he was unable to get to the house the last time he tried. "I'll see."

"If you can, that would be great. Just having that would tell you what you wanted to know. And I guess what you want to know is that this person is real and not a figment of your overworked imagination. Is that what we're trying to prove here?"

"I suppose so, Lavern. I'm not real sure anymore."

"Anyway, the truth of the matter is that some people have gone through life never needing a birth certificate. They got a job, got married, got a driver's license, and were never asked for it. Have you ever been asked for your birth certificate?"

"Come to think of it, no, I haven't."

"And you probably never will be unless you try to get a passport. That's the one time it usually comes up."

"How about a social security card? Don't you need one to get a number?"

"Nope."

"Then how about a marriage license? "

"Nope."

"I don't mean do you need a birth certificate to get one. I mean isn't there some record at the license bureau if she got married?"

"*If* she got married. And then, what county or city or small town? It may take you weeks to research all that. And what do you have when you're through?"

"I would have proof that this woman lived. Or maybe proof that she died. Okay, let's say she was born in the mountains with no record of her birth and she never got married, but if she died, there has to be a death certificate."

"If she's dead." Lavern looked him coldly in the eye. "J. D., I don't think she's dead."

A chill went through him that even Marge's coffee couldn't warm. He felt the hairs on his arms and neck tingle. Lizzie Clem might still be alive and living somewhere in this very town. He put his elbows on the table and his face in both his hands. He could feel his heart beating in his chest and temples, and he had to swallow before he spoke.

"Have you tried anything as simple as a phone book?"

"All the major cities in the southeast. Again, it will take weeks to check the entire country. And then they, too, are unreliable at best. You have unlisted numbers and unpublished numbers and, worst of all, cell phones. Do you realize how many people don't have land lines in their homes anymore?"

J. D. wanted to say something, but his throat was dry and yielding to the dullness he felt in his brain. He began a sentence, but then thought better of it. "What about ..."

"What about what?"

"I was just thinking about those pop-ups you get on the computer all time about finding old classmates or old boyfriends. What about those things?"

"You ever tried it?" she asked.

"No, I can't say that I have."

"Most of them are games. Remember, it's the Internet."

They sat in silence, deep in thought. J. D. refilled his cup, and Lavern shook off the offer. They listened without hearing the old music that was playing on the sound system in the back office. It was J. D.'s favorite kind of music. The Pied Pipers were singing Johnny Mercer's "Dream." Lavern never took her eyes off him.

"There's something you're not telling me," she said.

"Yeah. I went back out there yesterday evening. The bridge was gone. I couldn't get across."

"Try again."

"Do you want to go with me?"

"I thought you had to go alone."

"So did I, but I *was* alone and nothing happened. But … I don't know. Maybe two people who believe will have better luck. I'm willing to try anything."

"Thanks, but I don't think so. I don't feel like the trip. You go. And if you fail again, accept that it was meant to be. The Mission is over."

"That's the very word I thought of, but … it's not enough. I have to know why. And in order to find that out, I have to know for sure the Clems are real."

"J. D. Wickman, you're a stubborn man. But that's part of your charm. Don't ever give it up. As for me, I'm going home. I'll call you if anything comes up."

And she was gone.

J. D. left shortly after and headed for the bridge. He had driven the van this morning and had transferred the chicken feed and tobacco and books and hoe from the TR3 just in case. Maybe he *had* hit on something about the faith of two people being stronger than that of one, but without Lavern, there was no way to know. His only chance now was to hope yesterday was an anomaly. Perhaps he would drive right across that one lane bridge the way he had the first time. *Yeah,* he thought to himself, *just like the first time.*

Chapter Twenty-three

As bad as Friday night had been, the worst of his life, Saturday night wasn't much better. He and Karlie hardly spoke. The only words exchanged between them were about Angela. She had called and told Karlie what a wonderful time she'd had at the mixer and how glad she was to be back at school. Whatever metamorphosis had taken place in her young heart or mind was certainly welcome. At least his daughter was happy. He only wished he and his wife were. Maybe when all of this was over, things would get back to normal, and they would never have to talk or think about it again. Sadly, he couldn't imagine a time when he wouldn't think about it. It was becoming a growing, indelible pain that he feared would be a memory he'd take to his grave. How could he ever forget the pallid

and sickly face of Lizzie Clem lying on those yellowed sheets? Or
the squint of Paul Clem's eyes when he said, "You're a slick one, ain't
you?" These and other images gave way to few moments of rest as
he lay in bed, fitfully trying to make sense of it all. He found himself praying, hard and desperately, for a solution—for comfort—for
peace of mind. He resigned in his heart that only God could rescue
him from the misery and confusion he had been thrust into.

The phone startled him awake. It was as if the ring was clang-
ing inside his head instead of just next to it. He glanced quickly at
the alarm clock on the nightstand: 5:10 a.m. He sat straight up. He
thought of his mother—had something happened? He grabbed it
and nearly shouted, "Hello."

Karlie was awake and asking, "Who is it? Who is it?"

J. D. waved her off and listened intently. If someone was saying
anything on the other end, he certainly couldn't hear it. He repeated,
"Hello? Hello?" each time a little louder than before. And then finally
he heard the voice.

"J. D.," Lavern Justice said with no apology in her tone for calling at such an hour. "Do you take the Fayetteville paper?"

"No."

"Then go online and call it up. The obits. I'll talk to you later."

The line went dead, and he sat there in bed with his brain
scrambled.

"Who was that?"

"A woman I know."

"A woman? At five o'clock in the morning? What is going on,
J. D.?"

"Nothing. Not what you think, anyway."

"What woman?"

"Her name is Lavern Justice. You don't know her. She's an older woman."

"And why is she calling my house and my husband at five o'clock in the morning?"

"You wouldn't understand. Just let it go."

"Let it go, you say. Would you if some man was calling me at home in the middle of the night?"

"It's not the middle of the night, Karlie. You just said yourself, it's five o'clock in the morning. She's a woman who has been helping me with some research."

J. D. said all this while getting out of bed and putting on his pants and shirt.

He stopped just before leaving the room and looked at his distraught wife, who was now sitting against the headboard with both hands to her mouth. All he could see was the hurt and fear in her eyes.

"I promise you, honey, there's no reason to worry. It's about what's been going on. Something's up. I don't know what, but I need to go to the computer. I'll tell you all about it later." He turned and left the room and then ran down the stairs taking two steps at a time. He went to the basement and hit one button that started the whirr and the other one that lit up the screen. All he could think of was that DSL should be faster than this.

He typed in *Fayetteville Observer,* and when the home page popped up, he looked for obituaries. He paused just a moment, the cursor hovering over the word. His heart was racing. He took a deep breath and clicked.

The accounts of all city and surrounding-area deaths were apparently in alphabetical order. He scrolled each one of them. The first was Acord. Then Bell and Bosserman. Friedman. Hanger. He scrolled slowly through to the last one, Walker, and still didn't see what he was supposed to be looking for. Twenty-one deaths in all, but no Clem. He started from the top again, and this time he scanned each one, looking for a clue. There was nothing until he got to the Ss. And there it was. Elizabeth Clem Stockendale. All the air went out of his chest, and a pain shot between his shoulder blades. He took a deep breath and slowly read every word.

> *Elizabeth Clem Stockendale*
>
> > *Fayetteville—Elizabeth Ann (Clem) Stockendale, 81, of 327 Holyoke Lane, went to see the Lord at 2:25 p.m. on Thursday, September 13, 2007 at her home. She was the widow of Robert Mason Stockendale, who preceded her in death in August of 1952.*
> >
> > *She was born on April 4, 1926 in Norge Springs, North Carolina, a daughter of the late Paul C. and Ada L. Clem.*
> >
> > *Mrs. Stockendale was a teacher in the Missouri school system for forty-one years and retired in 1995. She married Robert Stockendale in the summer of 1947 in West Plains, Missouri, and after his death in 1952 during the Korean Conflict, she attended Warten State Teacher's College and received her degree in English. She retired to her home state and enjoyed*

gardening, reading, and her best friend—her dog, Champ.

In addition to her parents and her husband, she was preceded in death by a brother, Carl Alton Clem, who was aboard the USS Arizona *at Pearl Harbor. She is survived by one niece, Lucille Clem Tanner— husband George C. Tanner; two great nieces, Patsy Boyer and Colleen Hiezer; two great-grand nieces, Linda Boyer and Cathy Boyer; and one great-grand nephew, Lyle Hiezer.*

There will be no visitation or funeral service at the request of the deceased. The body will be cremated.

He read it all again. And then again. Now he knew why he couldn't cross over yesterday and the day before. It was all over. He had sat along the road yesterday evening with all those items from the Barn and Farm store in his van and just stared at the spot where the house had been. Something had told him he would never cross over again. He felt that somewhere down deep where you feel fear and anxiety. And these words on a flickering computer monitor explained why. Lizzie was already dead.

He drew his eyes back to the time of death. 2:25 p.m. Thursday. It must have been just minutes after he left the farmhouse for the last time. Just minutes after he sat in the dusty lane and saw something move past the shades in the upstairs window. Maybe that *wasn't* Paul. Maybe it was Lizzie. But he knew this for certain. The medicine had worked. He had saved her life. He didn't know how it all happened or why, but he did know he couldn't stop here. He still needed

answers. He had to know what was being kept from him. By God
Himself. And he knew before he even got up from his chair that he
was going to Fayetteville.

→

He left the house long before he had to. The drive would only take
two hours, but he didn't want to hang around any longer than necessary. Karlie wasn't speaking to him at all, and he was in no condition
to explain things to her—and even if he were, she was in no condition to hear it. So he drove out of town and stopped for breakfast,
mulling it all over in his mind again and again until his temples
ached. He drove well below the speed limit all the way, more in tune
with his thoughts than with the road.

He knew his way around Fayetteville a little but not enough to
find a house in a residential district. He stopped at a gas station and
asked where Holyoke Lane was.

"How do you spell that?"

"H-o-l-y-o-k-e."

"That's a new one on me, pal."

"Then do you have a city map?"

"Let me see." The man behind the counter fumbled with a lot of
papers. "I've got a state map and a county map and … no. No city
map."

"Then where could I buy one on a Sunday morning?"

"Oh, you wanna *buy* one? Right back there on that rack."

J. D. smiled to himself and walked out with a city map. He sat under the steering wheel and unfolded it to its fullest size. He scanned the index, and there it was. *Holyoke Ln. E6.* He put one finger on E and the other on 6, and sure enough, when they met he couldn't find Holyoke anywhere. This seemed to happen every time he tried to read a map. So he just focused on a small section in the area and looked intently until he saw the little dead-end street that was a lot closer to F7 than it was E6.

The traffic was mercifully thin. It was church time on a sunny Sunday, and he figured most everyone was either in the sanctuary of their choice or on their porch reading the paper or in the mountains or the lakes for the weekend. He was probably the only person in the whole town looking for the home of a woman he had read about in the obituaries that morning. Two more rights should have him at 327 Holyoke, but then what? He wasn't sure why, but he had to at least see the house where she had lived. He envisioned himself walking around the yard. He knew that could lead to an arrest, but with the state and the mood he was in this morning, he was willing to risk it.

There it was! On the left. A small white frame house. He slowed to a crawl and then finally stopped in the middle of the street. A short front yard just off the sidewalk. Two steps up to a porch with a lounge chair and a swing. In the back he could see a fenced-in yard. That had to be for Champ. There were flowers everywhere. Every kind imaginable that would still be in bloom in early September. She obviously loved color, and the beds around the sides of the house were peppered with blues and yellows and reds. To the right was a short driveway and ... why hadn't he seen that immediately?

In the driveway was a car. A green Ford that looked less than two years old. Was this hers? Had she still been driving at eighty-one? Or did it belong to someone who was inside? His questions were answered almost as if he had asked them out loud, because at that instant a woman, looking to be in her late sixties, came bouncing out the back door and put a large box in the trunk of the Ford Five Hundred.

Chapter Twenty-four

J. D. drove to the end of the dead-end street and turned around, giving himself a little more time to come up with a good story about who he was and why he was here. He wanted to have it all planned out in his head before he walked up and introduced himself to the woman loading the car. He just needed some time to figure out what he was going to say. By the time he had come back up the street and was pulling to the curb in front of the little white house, he still had no idea. So he just turned off the engine, got out, and walked up the couple of steps to the front porch. He had come this far not knowing what he was doing, so why stop now?

Just as his foot hit the porch, the front door flew open, and a huge golden retriever took a leap and hit him in the chest with two enormous front paws. J. D. laughed, grabbing the dog with both hands and ruffling the hair on top of his head. "Hey, boy! You nearly knocked me over."

The dog panted and smiled and panted some more, and J. D. was instantly on his knees, rubbing the dog's head vigorously. The woman who had been loading the car a few minutes before came rushing out and said, "I think Champ likes you, mister. He's such a friendly pup and so full of energy." And then, in the same breath, she changed the direction of her one-sided conversation and said to the dog, "Leave the man alone, Champ." And then to J. D, "I hope you like dogs, 'cause that dog sure does like you."

J. D. looked up at her and, never taking his hands off the animal, said, "I love dogs, and he's a pretty one."

"My name is Lucille Tanner. Are you a neighbor? We don't live around here, so we don't know many of Auntie Liz's neighbors, but she sure had some good ones. They all looked in after her and saw to her needs. Some really good people in this neighborhood. Where do you live? Next door? I think that's the cutest house next door. You'll have to tell me where you got that porch awning. It reminds me of a house we had at the beach one time."

J. D. was digesting the situation almost as fast as Lucille was talking. Not quite, but almost. This must be Lizzie's niece. If he underplayed his part just enough, Lucille's constant, breathless chatter could work to his advantage. Keep her talking, and he could find out everything he needed to know.

"So which house is yours?"

"Well, none of them actually. I don't live in this neighborhood."

"Oh. How did you know Auntie Liz? She had so many friends. People just seemed to take to her. All kinds of people."

"Yes, ma'am. I'm just a friend."

"Well, I know it's a little soon, but we're going to get this house ready to put on the market. Just as soon as we get some of this stuff cleaned out inside. My husband, George, is in there now. He's started in the attic, and I have never seen such a mess. Mind you, I loved my Auntie Liz, but I do believe she saved everything she ever owned. Get down, Champ. Leave the man alone."

"He's not bothering me. I love dogs."

"I love 'em, too, but I don't want 'em all over me. She never disciplined her animals, but she loved this one. Took good care of 'im. I have to say that. You're a friend of Auntie Liz's. You say you're not a neighbor. You knew her well?"

"Well, yes. I knew her and thought the world of her."

"She was a good woman, wasn't she? Everybody who ever met her just loved her to death. And she had so many students all those years she taught that she kept up with. They would call her and write to her, and they always sent Christmas cards. I just don't know how I'll ever get the word to all of them that she's passed. I was thinking about putting a piece in the paper out there in Missouri or something like that. You know, just to let them know. They all thought so much of her. How did you know her then? And what's your name?"

Lucille was making J. D. dizzy. The number of subjects she could cover in one take was putting him in a fog. He wasn't sure he could think fast enough to dodge this ole gal.

"My name's J. D. Wickman. And I was real sorry to see in the paper this morning about your aunt."

"We knew it was coming, but you know, you're still never pre-pared for these sort of things. I'm all the real family she has left. She only had the one brother. That was my father. He was older than she was, and he died at Pearl Harbor. I never knew him. He was shipped out before I was even born. Before the war even started. It was just them two. My daddy and Auntie Liz. And when she got married and moved out to the west she never had much family out there either. Her husband, now, his name was Bob Stockendale, he was killed in the war just like my daddy. A different war, but still just the same. I only saw him once, I think. They were only married for a few years, and then there she was all those years by herself. Never remarried. Should have. I told her all the time she should have. We used to write real regular, and I told her she needed a man. But Auntie Liz—boy, she had a mind of her own. What's your name again?"

"Wickman. J. D."

"What's that stand for? That J. D.?"

"John David."

"I like that better. I'll just call you John. That's easier. My hus-band had a cousin they called B. B., and I thought that was the silliest thing I ever heard. I just called him Bob. I never knew what the Bs even stood for, but I just called him Bob. Auntie Liz did a lot of charity work at the library here after she retired. She loved books. Loved to read. She's got rooms full of books in there. I don't know what we're going to do with all of them. Is that where you knew her from? The library?"

"Yes." J. D. knew if he was just patient and waited, Lucille would provide his cover for him, and she did.

"I think Champ really likes you. Don't know what we're going to do with him either. We live up in Virginia, and we can't take him. George has huntin' dogs, and I don't think they'd mix. That's why we can't stay more than a couple of days. We've got dogs and grandchildren up there. I hope we can get all this mess cleaned up in a couple of days. We'll have to come back for the sale. Heaven knows when that will be. There's just so much to do, and I guess I'm not getting much of it done standing out here talking to you. Do you want to come in?"

"Sure. I'll help pack things up if you would like for me to."

"We can always use another hand." She opened the screen door, and they went inside, the dog leading the way. "This is the living room. This is where the neighbor across the street found her. Bless her heart, she was sitting right there in that chair, reading one of her novels. She loved mysteries. And it was as if she had just fallen asleep. The neighbor was bringing her mail in, and she knocked on the door, and when Auntie Liz didn't answer, she looked in the window and saw her just sitting there as if she'd fallen asleep. Peaceful-like. What a sweet way of goin'. She called the ambulance, you know, the rescue squad, and they broke the lock and came on in. But she was gone when they got here. Just slept away. Heart attack, I guess. That's how they came up with the time of death. They figured she'd been dead about thirty minutes by the time they got to her. George! George!" she yelled up the steps. "He can't hear me. He must be in the attic."

Her attention was quickly back on J. D. "For instance, here's an old box of pictures we found this morning. I don't know who any of these people are. I never knew any of my family. Never even knew my grandmother or my grandfather for that matter. I might have seen him once, but I can't clearly remember." All the time she was talking, she was handing the pictures to J. D., and he was leafing through them. "Now, that one I'm pretty sure must have been my grandfather, even though there's nothing written on the back."

J. D. looked at the tall, thin figure in the three-piece suit and saw Paul Clem staring back at him, his foot raised on the bumper of a 1936 Chevy. Before he thought, he said, "Yeah, that's him all right."

"What? You didn't know him did you? Of course you didn't. How old are you, son?" Then she chuckled.

"No." J. D. faked a laugh while cold perspiration broke out on his neck. "I just meant Lizzie looked exactly like him."

"Lizzie. Funny you should say that. No one called her that anymore. Did she tell you to call her that? Because she was always Miss Elizabeth to all her students and friends. But speaking of my grandfather. I said I never knew him. Did you know what happened to him? Did she ever tell you?"

"No, she never said much about him."

"I'm not surprised. I mean, I think he was a good man and all, but he had a lot on him. Lost his wife, then lost a son in the war, and one day he just took a shotgun and went upstairs in the front room and ended it all. Shot himself in the head, and nobody at home except poor Auntie Liz—and she was just a teenaged girl at the time."

J. D. froze at the memory of seeing that final image in the upstairs bedroom. Was the movement he saw really Paul, and could it have been …? He was afraid to finish his thought.

"Right in the house. What a shame. What a crying shame for poor Auntie Liz. It was no wonder she never talked about it. Here are some empty boxes, John. You can pack those books over there and all those knickknacks. She had oodles, didn't she? This was the room she lived in most. I think there were nights she never even went up to bed. She just slept in that chair. Everything she needed was right here at her fingertips. The TV, a radio, her sewing basket, all those books. And look. Here's her little Bible they gave her when she was in grade school. A little New Testament. Do you have any idea how old that is?"

"Yeah, I think I do," J. D. said, absently touching the ragged corners.

"You just make yourself at home. I'll go up and help George. He falls sometimes. Has trouble with his balance, and he's got no business up there in that attic by himself."

And as Lucille's voice trailed off going up the steps, J. D. knelt down and rubbed Champ's head again. He needed a minute to think about Paul and the shadow at the window, but he was having trouble processing everything that was being thrown at him. He looked around the room and found it hard to believe that the old woman who had just died here three days ago was the same teenaged girl he had just talked to three days ago. The air was suddenly thick, and his emotions almost too much for him to handle. Champ saved the day when he licked him on the side of the face and brought him back to reality.

J. D. stood and walked around the chair. He looked at the pictures on the wall. Landscapes and flowers. No family portraits or snapshots. The curtains were old and dark, and the room-size rug was worn at the edges. The books ranged from the classics to the mysteries Lucille said her aunt loved. There was everything from Chaucer and Twain to Erle Stanley Gardner and Ngaio Marsh. They were all arranged in alphabetical order according to authors. He looked through the Cs, and sure enough, there was a hardback copy of Agatha Christie's *The Body in the Library.* The same book he still had in the back of the van. He had made a good choice after all. He said aloud, "I knew you'd like that book, Lizzie."

"Did you say something?"

J. D. turned quickly and saw whom he assumed to be George standing at the bottom of the stairs.

"You must be George Tanner. I'm John Wickman."

"My wife said you were down here. I'm on my way to the basement. She's still upstairs. Tell her where I am if she comes down. And don't let her talk your leg off."

"I'll do my best."

J. D. sat down in Lizzie's chair. The chair she had died in. He looked across the room at the nineteen-inch TV and the lamp sitting beside it and filled his mind with the idea that he was seeing the final things she had seen just before she closed her eyes for the last time. Champ came and put his chin in J. D.'s lap. With one hand J. D. rubbed the dog's head, and with the other he reached down and picked up the TV listing insert she had kept on the floor by her chair. Under the paper was an old tan sewing basket. He picked up the basket with his free hand and put it in his lap. He opened it. *It's strange,* he thought, *how we all keep close to us the things we love the most. The things that tell our life stories.*

He reached inside the basket, and among the threads and buttons and thimbles and little packs of needles, he picked up some old campaign buttons. One for somebody named Turner who had run for the Senate in Missouri. A Truman button from 1948. Two movie tickets to the Rialto. This could have been the last movie she and Robert had gone to see together. Coins. Some nickels and dimes and some old eagle half-dollars. A picture in a small silver frame of a man in uniform standing in front of a tank. Robert, again, he was sure. There were a couple of keys, maybe to the house but probably to nothing. Keys often have a way of outstaying their usefulness and even their memory. He looked at a picture of a small country church, and on the border she had written "Easter Sunday 1953." And in the very bottom of the basket was something yellow he couldn't quite make out. He dug with his one hand, still stroking Champ's head, and touched something round and plastic. He picked it up and recognized it immediately. It was a pill bottle, and the faint, faded letters, almost unreadable with age, said, *Dr. N. Annata—J. D. Wickman—Amoxicillin.* And it was dated three days ago. *September 13, 2007.*

J. D. began to cry. And he was still crying when Lucille came down the steps. She went to him and hugged him and said, "That's okay, honey. We all loved her so very much, didn't we?"

Chapter Twenty-five

The two-hour drive home from Fayetteville was the shortest trip J. D. had ever made. He was aware of nothing the entire way, and when he reached Hanson, he had no memory of any part of it. He had been on autopilot since he pulled away from the curb in front of Elizabeth Stockendale's house—or, more precisely, from the moment he had reached into that old wicker sewing basket and touched a small plastic bottle that had traveled through and bridged time in a way he still could not fathom. His mind was numb, slipping in and out of reality, trying to register what had happened to him in the past six days. He attempted to piece it all together as the road signs and mile markers whizzed past his windshield. And it was truly as if they were going past him instead of the other way around.

He had no sense of movement or control. And no matter how much he tried to make it all fit, the one word that kept haunting him was *why*. The *what* scared him to death. The *how* puzzled him. But the *why* haunted and ate at him like a hungry demon. He had to talk to someone.

Karlie was his first choice, but he knew it would only drive her further away. She didn't understand what had happened to him— and how could he blame her? After all, her stand was the rational and conventional one. Ask a hundred random people on the street, and they would all agree with her that he needed psychiatric help. And then there was Jack. His oldest and dearest friend, who'd been with him through boyhood scrapes and teenage dreams and neighborhood pranks and all of life's problems. They had a bond that couldn't be broken with sword or hammer. But this … this had broken it. He could see it on Jack's face. Jack doubted him. Jack had never doubted him before. This was a first. And how could he blame him, either? He had to admit that it *did* sound like the rantings of a madman.

There was only one place he could go, and he suddenly realized he was already headed in that direction. He turned down his second dead-end street for the day. How peculiar that Lizzie and Lavern both lived on a dead-end street.

J. D. walked up the short pathway to the front door and banged the brass door knocker three times. After about twenty seconds, he did it again. He looked at his watch and saw it was almost five thirty. He had stayed a lot longer in Fayetteville than he meant to, but helping Lucille and George clean out some of the rooms had been a comfort to him, and he felt a little closer to Lizzie the longer he stayed. Lucille and George told him to come back tomorrow if he liked, as they wouldn't leave until sometime Tuesday. He told them he might and meant it.

He was about to knock one last time when he heard a voice from behind him. "Can I help you?"

He turned and saw a woman of seventy-plus years in what he could only describe as church clothes. But then, it *was* Sunday evening.

"I'm sorry. You startled me. I was looking for Lavern."

"I'm her next-door neighbor, Ruth Lamossto." She held out her hand to be shaken.

J. D. accommodated her and said, "My name's J. D. I'm a friend of hers."

"Well, I'm afraid she's not at home, J. D.," Mrs. Lamossto said sweetly.

"Do you know when she'll be back?"

"Haven't you heard?" she said even more sweetly and this time with concern in her voice.

"Heard what?"

"Lavern had a stroke. She's in the hospital in a coma, and it doesn't look good."

"What! A stroke? When? When did this happen?"

"Oh, it must have been ..." Ruth Lamossto squinted and raised her eyes to the treetops as if the answer might be there and said, "It must have been ten days ago."

"No!" J. D. almost shouted. "It couldn't have been ten days ago I just talked to her...." But he never finished the sentence with his lips; only in his mind. *I just talked to her this morning. And I've only known her since Tuesday.*

"I think I'm right about that," Ruth said with conviction. "This is Sunday, and it was on a … let me see … yes, it was. It was exactly ten days ago."

J. D. felt an urgent need to sit down. His knees would no longer hold him. He found a chair a few steps away on the small front porch and leaned on it. Ruth continued to talk.

"I've seen your car over here a couple of times this week. I thought you were family or a friend checking on the house for her. I can't imagine you didn't know."

It didn't even cross his mind to try to explain anything to this woman. So much had happened that he didn't understand; he was past thinking anyone else would. He didn't even know why he asked the next question.

"Did you see me or just my car?"

Ruth looked a little shocked at the question, but she answered him. "I saw your vehicle out front twice, and then I saw you coming up the walk. Then a few minutes later I saw you leave. I'm not nosy. The only reason I came over just now was because you kept knocking on her door where before you didn't. Before, you just went on in."

There was so much more he wanted to ask but was afraid to. The sensory overload might put him over the top.

"What hospital is she at? Here at the General?"

"Oh, no. They took her right on to Raleigh. I haven't been over because I just don't like to drive that far anymore, but I've talked to her nephew, and he says it's just a matter of time. She hasn't been awake since it happened. Ten days now in a coma. It's such a shame. And there's no reason to drive over there. They're not letting anyone in to see her."

J. D. walked to his car without saying good-bye or thank you. Ruth Lamossto stood in her neighbor's yard and watched him get in the car and drive away. He was certain she was staring at his license plate.

$\rightarrow$

J. D. had never felt more alone. The one ally who believed him and believed *in* him was gone. Whoever she was, she had guided him through everything when those closest to him wouldn't even talk to him. She had become some sort of angelic chaperon to see him through this most difficult and confusing time. But how ... and what was she ...? Hadn't she said once she was very spiritual? He began examining his short but very personal relationship with Lavern. The facts chilled him.

She had always known when he was not being truthful. That Light in her eye. There was something she'd said to him ... about seeing things that aren't there. "No. If you see it, it's there. Think of it as dimensions. Not illusions," she'd said. But what about Dr. Annata? Come to think of it, neither he nor his staff ever really acknowledged that they knew J. D. was coming that day. Maybe Lavern just knew Annata was a pill pusher and anyone with fifty dollars could charm their way in and get what they wanted. And the phone calls. He had always answered the phone himself at home. Karlie never actually talked to her, and he was sure Lavern's voice wouldn't actually be on his answering machine. He was afraid to ask Marge or anyone at the west-end restaurant about it. He had a pretty good idea what they would say. That he was sitting in that booth alone, drinking coffee with a second empty cup across the table from him. They would all probably agree with Karlie and Jack that his next stop should be a hospital room of his own.

And maybe they were right.

There were just too many things that would never make sense to a right-thinking person. And no matter how hard he tried to reason out each situation, he just couldn't find sanity in the solution. It was time to see the doctor Karlie had wanted him to see from the very beginning. He was ready to resign himself to that fate. Or *nearly* ready.

There was still one place he could go. One person who wouldn't turn him away or doubt him.

Chapter Twenty-six

He wasn't sure how long he had been there, but he noticed that the sun was beginning its descent. The room, facing the west, had lost its evening glow, and the lamp on the mahogany nightstand was quickly becoming the brightest light in the room. He and his mother were on their third game of checkers. She had won the first, and he had won the second. He remembered this was how it always turned out when he was a little boy and she played with him in front of the TV on Sunday nights. She would always let him win one and then lose one so that the third game would really feel like a championship. For all he knew, she was doing the same thing tonight.

"I don't know what possessed you to come over on a Sunday night, but I'm sure glad you did. Does this mean you're not coming Tuesday?"

"No. I'll still be here Tuesday. And if you let me win this game, I may even come back Friday."

They both laughed, and she took two of his men. Without looking up from the board she asked, "What is it, J. D.? What's on your heart?"

"Nothing, Mom. I'm fine."

"I can see it in your eyes and your whole face. Are you well?"

"Yes, I promise you, I am. I know you told Angela you thought I might be sick, but I assure you I'm okay. And speaking of Angela, what did you tell her that made her go back to school?"

"Oh," Beatrice said innocently, "did I say something that nudged her in that direction?"

"Yeah. She told us some story about me wanting to quit and wait on Karlie to graduate from high school and how you and Dad both had a problem adjusting to college life. You and Dad never went to college did you?"

"Now, J. D. I never actually said you quit school. I didn't tell her how it turned out. I was just letting her know that she wasn't alone in the feelings she was having. That's all."

"So the end justifies the means, and little white lies fall by the crimson path and all that stuff, huh?"

"You have such a nice way of putting it, J. D. It's your move."

He took one of her men.

"Is it Karlie?" she asked.

"Is what Karlie?"

"The thing that you're worried about. Is there a problem with you and her?"

"No, Mom. I told you. It's not anything. It's not anything that has anything to do with family."

"It's those restaurants, isn't it? Two are just too many."

"And no, it's not the restaurants. Business is fine, and so is everything else. And as soon as one of us wipes off this board, I've got to get out of here. Karlie will think I left her."

She took two more men and leaned back against her pillow. The game was over. J. D. stood up, leaned down to kiss her cheek, and said he would call in a couple of days. He wiggled her toe through the sheet with his fingers as he walked past the foot of her bed.

"I love you, Mom."

"I love you, too. I only wish you trusted me."

"I trust you."

"Whenever you need to talk, I'm always here."

J. D. stopped in the doorway. He looked at his mother and saw the sincerity in her face and promised her, "Mom. I'll tell you all about it one day. Right now I don't feel like talking about it. But maybe ... Mom, let me ask you one thing before I go."

"Anything, honey."

He knew it was a long shot, but they were of the same age and same generation, and she wanted to help—so why not?

"Mom," J. D. said as he sat back down on the straight chair by the bed, "did you ever know a woman by the name of Lizzie Clem?"

"Clem? No. No. Never knew a Clem named Lizzie."

"Or maybe Elizabeth?"

"No. That either. I don't think so."

"How about an Elizabeth Stockendale?"

"Elizabeth Stockendale. No, I don't think so."

J. D. sighed. He'd given it a try. He hadn't thought there was much chance his mother could help, but he had made an effort and, bless her heart, so had she.

"Now, I knew a *Beth* Stockendale."

"What did you say?"

"Beth Stockendale. That could be short for Elizabeth, couldn't it?"

"Yes, it could. How did you know her?" J. D.'s heart was leaping from his chest again. He was sure his face was as white as the sheets on his mother's bed.

"Don't you remember her? No, I guess you wouldn't. But you do remember that summer when you were ten years old, don't you? You and your sister had ridden your bicycles up to the grocery store for ice cream, and, stubborn as you both were, you tried to ride home eating your Popsicle with one hand and steering with the other. I shudder just thinking about all of it again."

J. D. remembered all of this very well. He shuddered too.

"Well, as you were pulling out into the street, you turned right in front of a car, and it hit you and sent you flying. There you were, lying in the middle of the road, bleeding from the head, your sister hysterical, and your father and I at home with no idea of what was going on. Traffic stopped and lined up on both sides of the streets. Someone called the rescue squad, and your sister took off running home to tell us what had happened. You were unconscious. Unconscious and bleeding."

Much of this story was vivid to J. D., but he couldn't sort out what came from his memory and what came from all the family retellings of it.

"There was a lady in one of the cars lined up in traffic, she was from out of state, and she ran to you and sat down in the road and cradled your head in her arms, waiting for the ambulance. But it didn't come. They waited for I don't how long; so many different people told me the story later. She finally said to one of the drivers of another car, "We've got to get this boy to a hospital. Do you know where one is?" and the man said he did, and she grabbed you up in her arms and sat in the back seat of that man's car and held your head. When they got to the emergency room they said she carried you in by herself. Wouldn't let anyone else touch you till the doctor got there. And then the doctor got there and got you all fixed up—you do remember that you were in the hospital for three days and two nights, don't you?"

"Oh, yeah, I remember that."

"Well, when that doctor, Dr. Corbett, got you fixed up—by that time your daddy and I were there—he told us that if that woman hadn't brought you in when she did that he couldn't guarantee you would have lived. It was that bad and that close. He was mad as a hornet at the rescue squad. The woman who carried you—the woman who saved your life—her name was Beth Stockendale. She was just passing through and happened to be right there, or you might not be here tonight."

J. D.'s throat was paralyzed, and his mouth couldn't form the words he wanted to say. When his mother asked, "Don't you remember your daddy and me mentioning her name?" all he could do was shake his head no.

"She called every day for a week and checked on you. Such a sweet woman. But she lived out in the Midwest somewhere—Kansas or Missouri. I don't remember anymore. We wrote letters back and forth for a while because I was so grateful to her and what she had done. We would trade Christmas cards, and she always asked about you. 'How is my beautiful little John?' she would say. She always called you John. But then as time went on, we sort of lost contact with one another, and I'm so sorry we did. I think about her often."

Lizzie knew! She knew that boy she saved was the man who had saved *her* life when she was a teenager. She had the pill bottle with his name on it and the date. She had kept it all those years, and when she learned who the unconscious boy in the hospital was … she *had* to know. And then one day, she moved back and lived so close but never contacted him. He wondered if she had come in his restaurant and eaten dinner and watched him. Or driven by his house the way he had driven by hers. Or maybe she was afraid it would upset the dimensions. Isn't that what Lavern had called them? Dimensions?

And now he knew the *why.* Why all of this had happened. He had saved Lizzie's life so she could save his. And Lizzie had saved his life so he could save hers. His head spun at the implications until he landed on a singular truth: *We're all connected in God's universe, even across generations. And we're all in need of one another.*

His mother squeezed his hand there in the twilight and, as if she could read his mind, said, "He does work His mysteries, J. D. He does work His mysteries."

And J. D. Wickman knew his hard and desperate prayers had been heard, handled, and answered. Answered by the Architect of Time, a grace-filled and caring God.

Epilogue

It was another glorious, late-summer Monday morning. Just cool enough outside not to need the air conditioning on and just warm enough to warrant having all the windows thrown open. J. D. had gotten up early, and when Karlie came down the steps at seven thirty ready for her day, he was standing, fully dressed, in front of the brewing coffee and buttered toast. He handed her a cup as he was just getting off the phone.

"Absolutely. Yes. Yes. By noon. I promise you. Good-bye."

He hung up the phone and said, "Your breakfast is ready."

"Thank you," she said cautiously, a puzzled but thankful smile on her face.

J. D. was full of life, and the early, blinding sunshine coming through the windows gave him energy. "Honey, I know things have been less than perfect around here lately. But that's all in the past. I just want to say I love you very much. More than life itself. And I want to ask you to do me a favor today."

"And I might ask you to do me one. Like see Dr. Maxton."

"I really don't think that's going to be necessary now, babe."

"Well, I do. You should see the doctor, then maybe we should take a vacation and try to solve some of the things that are haunting you."

"Just listen, Karlie, and give me the benefit of the doubt. I know that's asking a lot, but I promise you are never going to see the same ole J. D. you've been putting up with for the past week. Trust me. If I'm lying, I'll move *in* with Dr. Maxton."

She looked at him, and he watched as her determination softened into a familiar, loving gaze. She sipped her coffee and said, "J. D., you know I'd go to the ends of the earth for you."

"Well, you won't have to go that far. But here's what I want you to do. Whatever you have planned today, cancel it. Wipe your calendar clean just this once. Give me this one day with no questions asked."

She laughed, obviously relieved to see him back to his old happy self. "What are we going to do?"

"I want you to go someplace with me."

She stiffened. "Not out to that bridge again?"

"No. Not out to that bridge. Never again out to that bridge."

"Okay, where to?"

"Get your purse and grab your coffee. We're leaving right now."

"Right now?" she laughed.

"Yes, and I promise you, once we leave here this morning, when we come back this house will never be the same again."

"What does that mean? And where are we going?"

He took her by the arm and led her toward the door. "We're going to Fayetteville."

"Fayetteville?" she repeated as she grabbed a sweater from the back of a chair.

He pushed her toward the door and closed and locked it behind him.

"Yeah, we're going there to pick up a friend. His name is Champ, and I think you're going to like him."

... a little more ...

When a delightful concert comes to an end,

the orchestra might offer an encore.

When a fine meal comes to an end,

it's always nice to savor a bit of dessert.

When a great story comes to an end,

we think you may want to linger.

And so, we offer ...

AfterWords—just a little something more after you

have finished a David C. Cook novel.

We invite you to stay awhile in the story.

Thanks for reading!

Turn the page for ...

- **Discussion Questions**
- **An Interview with Don Reid**

DISCUSSION QUESTIONS

Use these questions to spark conversation in your book club or readers' group.

1. What was your initial reaction to the characters in *One Lane Bridge?* Which character do you relate to most? Least?

2. What are some of J. D.'s best qualities? Worst? What are some of Karlie's best qualities? Worst?

3. What appeals to you about the setting of this story? Why is this sort of story best set in a small town? In what ways is the town itself a "character"?

4. What are the primary themes of the story? What messages did you discover as you read and thought about the story?

5. What is the greatest surprise in the story? What does this surprise teach you about the characters? About yourself?

6. What role does faith play in J. D.'s story?

7. In what ways do the Clems' needs affect J. D.'s priorities? How does J. D.'s relationship with the Clems affect his own family?

8. What insights into J. D.'s life do you get from the way he relates to his wife? What does this tell you about the sort of marriage he has?

9. What do you discover about J. D. through his relationship with his daughter, Angela?

10. What role does J. D.'s mother play in his story, and why is it such an important one?

11. What stands out to you about J. D.'s relationship with his best friend, Jack?

12. What is Lavern Justice's role in this story?

13. How is J. D.'s story a metaphor for faith? In what ways?

14. What does the one lane bridge symbolize?

15. What role does time play in *One Lane Bridge?* Why is that significant?

16. In what ways is this a story about God's "mysterious ways"? What does the story teach us about God? About trust?

AN INTERVIEW WITH DON REID

This is your second novel based in small-town America. What is it about small towns that makes them such a great setting for your stories?

I grew up in a small town. I love the big cities for an occasional visit, but I've never been tempted to become a part of one. Small towns give you close and personal relationships. You see the same faces on the streets each day. You get to know the people around you and their habits, and they become a part of your daily routine. You know when a baby is born or an old man dies, and you know the families—their needs and their cares. I still love walking the streets of Staunton, Virginia, the small town that I was born in and grew up in. Every person you meet on the sidewalk, every storefront, every corner, and every crossing has a story. Some real, some imagined. But there is always a peace and a drama in every block.

Tell us a bit about the specific inspiration for the protagonist of this novel, J. D. Wickman.

I wanted to write about a typical entrepreneur who was trying to establish himself in business and trying to be a loving husband, a responsible father, a loyal and thoughtful son, a good friend, and a substantial citizen to his hometown. And then this odd thing happens to him and stresses every relationship he has. We never know what's going to happen in the next minute or how we may react to it.

I just wanted to see an everyday guy reacting to an unusual situation. I don't think he handled it any better or any worse than you or I might. But I wanted to watch him go about his daily life with this on his mind. Sometimes I wasn't real sure how he would handle it from page to page until each situation manifested itself.

Which of the characters was most difficult for you to write, and why?

Maybe Karlie, J. D.'s wife. She loves him and is worried about him. And at the same time she disapproves of what he keeps inviting by taking those trips to the country. She's at odds with him at the restaurant and with their daughter, and yet she respects his perspective. She's the most complicated, the most giving, and the most understanding of all the characters. I always think the woman's story is going to be the hardest for me to write, and then I find it's not. But making sure she doesn't come off one-dimensional is the greatest challenge. Everyone is a mixture of right and wrong in attitude and action. And when writers tend to favor a gender or a race or a role model of some sort and make them forever perfect, I get really annoyed at that.

Which of the characters are you most like?

Oh, I guess I'd have to say J. D. I have to have answers. I'll go to any extreme to prove myself right or wrong. It's important to me to know for sure what I'm doing and why I'm doing it, to know what is happening around me and how it will affect me or the people I love. I take my religion on faith, but on worldly issues, I'm afraid I like answers. Just like J. D. If it meant going to the courthouse records or confiding in strangers who might help him solve his problem, he was willing to do it. We even share the same parenting techniques. J. D. and I are pretty soft when it comes to our children. And his moments with his mother were like moments I used to share with mine. And then there's Champ! Yeah, come to think of it, I guess ole J. D. and I are a lot alike.

What if, anything, surprised you about the story as it evolved?

I knew the plot from the beginning. So there were no surprises there. But what does tend to ambush me from time to time are the reactions of my characters. Until I get into the writing of a scene, I never know for sure just what they'll say, what inflection they may use—be it humor or sarcasm—or what actual words they may use. I don't know if they will be defensive or understanding when they are criticized or attacked. I don't know what their anger threshold is until it's tested with dialogue or with a particular adverse character. I love this about writing. Sometimes I am just as surprised as the reader when a gentle character suddenly turns harsh or a villainous type comes out with something sweet and endearing. Mary Sue Seymour, my literary agent, said to me just the other day in an email, "Isn't writing fun?" And, yes, I had to agree. Even when your brain gets tired and weary, it's still fun to see what's coming next.

Has your experience as a musician helped you as a novelist?

I think everything that has ever happened to you in life helps you as a novelist. From the most insignificant walk through a park to the most dramatic birth or traumatic death that is close to you, everything is another inroad to what makes you a novelist. I find myself recalling things from my past that I wasn't even aware of remembering in order to include that feeling in a paragraph. And as far as the music goes, of course there is no better bookmark to the past than a well-remembered and beautiful melody. The right song at the right time creates a mood and a retrospect that no amount of hard thinking could ever achieve. And what are songs if not just short stories that we piece together to make up our lives? I love combining the two: music and novels. Sometimes I'll put on an album from the period I'm writing in to give me the mood as I writing.

How do you come up with your ideas for your novels?

It all starts as just talking to myself in my head. I go to the track and walk. Usually Chipper, my dog, goes along, and I just think. I think of characters and situations and even conversations between characters. But I never write anything down. Not yet. This process may go on for weeks. If it leaves me, then I figure, good riddance. But if it remains and grows and piques my interest, then I carry it in my head for weeks. After a while, I'll write down the good ideas I've weeded out. Only when I feel sure this is good enough to be a book do I start writing the actual story. Those walks are also very important once I get into the story. That's where I rehearse the dialogue and the outlines for each chapter. (Chipper thinks I'm talking to him.)

Are you a plotter or a seat-of-the-pants writer? What is it about this approach that appeals to you?

As I've noted, I would have to say I'm both. I plot the big picture and then fly by the seat of my pants on the daily stuff. I know there are certain facts I have to get in the story line, but I'm not always sure just where they'll be. I know there is an end to my means but don't tie my hands on how I get there. It's like learning to sing a particular melody and then taking liberties with it and making it your own. I outline but not in the classical way. I have my own homegrown version of how I note what each chapter may reveal. You would need a code to read my notes. And sometimes, after those notes get cold, I wish I knew the code in order to decipher what I wrote.

When did you first know you wanted to be a novelist?

All my life. And I would have started sooner if I'd only had the time. I was in the music business from the time I was a teenager—singing, touring, writing songs, writing stage shows, writing TV shows, writing comedy routines. All that time I was an ardent reader but just didn't have the time to pursue writing. Now I do, and I'm loving every minute of it.

What's next after *One Lane Bridge?*

I'm going back to Mount Jefferson. The novel before this was called *O Little Town,* and it was set in Mount Jefferson, Virginia. The next book continues in that town with some of the characters from that book. It's called *The Mulligans of Mt. Jefferson.* I love the town and the folks that inhabit it. All I have to do is just walk the streets of my hometown, and I see those characters and their stories just come pouring out. I could write forever about those people who live in my town and in my head.

Also from Don Reid and David C. Cook

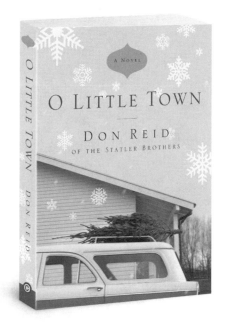

CHAPTER

From where I'm sitting, I can see where most of it took place. Down Main Street, clear to the end of the block, is where Macalbee's Five and Dime used to be. Then up this way, in the middle of the block, was the old police station. And if you look clear to the top of the hill, you can see the steeple from the Mason Street Methodist Church. Back then, if you listened carefully, you could hear the bell ring every morning at precisely nine o'clock—it was so dependable people opened their stores to it. And then right down there, of course, is the Crown Theater.

I don't remember the story from first-hand experience, of course, but I've heard it told often enough that it's almost as if I'd actually been there. It could have happened anywhere. In any town. In any state. But it happened in this town, Mt. Jefferson, and in a state of Christmas bustle like we haven't seen here in half a century. The sidewalks were overflowing with shoppers and the shoppers were overflowing with packages and snow was blowing and the Salvation Army ringers were ringing and people were filling their kettles. Elvis was on the radio, Ike was in the White House, and the Lord was in his holy temple. It was Christmas 1958.

❄

Actually it was two days before Christmas. Tuesday morning. 10:15. And it all started with a knock on the door of Milton Sandridge's second-floor office, which overlooked the sales floor of Macalbee's Five and Dime.

"Mr. Sandridge. Mr. Sandridge. It's urgent, Mr. Sandridge."

"Come in, Lois." Milton stood and walked around his desk, as he could tell by his assistant manager's voice something unusual was in the air.

As she opened the door, the look on her face matched the sound of her words. "We've got a shoplifter in aisle three."

They both turned and looked through the office window that gave an eagle's-eye view of everything and everybody in the store. Milton counted seven customers in aisle three. A mother with a baby in a stroller, a lone woman with a scarf tied under her chin, a colored woman with two small boys hanging on her coattail, and one teenage girl in jeans and a pea jacket. Milton looked back at Lois, shrugged, raised his eyebrows, and turned up the palms of his hands. She read his question and answered with the precision he always expected from her.

"The girl. Ponytail and dungarees. She's stuffing her pockets."

"Is somebody on the doors?"

"Ernest is watching both front doors and Tiny is watching the back."

"Do they know not to approach her until she hits the sidewalk?"

"They won't do anything till they hear from me. Or you."

"Have them stop her on the street. Take someone with you and bring her back to the storeroom and call the cops. You know the routine."

"Ah, there's a little more to it this time, I'm afraid."

"What do you mean?"

"Apparently you didn't get a good look at her. We know who she is."

"Lois, it's two days till Christmas. The store is filling up. We've got four people out with the flu and everything I ordered from the Sears catalog this year is late. Just tell me what's up. Who is she?"

"Millie Franklin."

"That's supposed to mean something to me?"

"Rev. Paul Franklin, up at the Methodist Church. His daughter."

This was the moment the palpitations started. That stuff about Sears and four people out with influenza and the store getting fuller by the minute didn't hold a candle to this. Millie Franklin. Why hadn't that name registered the first time he heard it? The season must have dulled his senses. But whatever it was going to take to awaken those senses now was going to have to happen in the next thirty seconds. Something had to be done before Millie got to the sidewalk because once she was there, she was a criminal, and there was nothing he could do about it.

Milton and Lois looked into each other's eyes and connected for only a second, then turned and squeezed through the office door at the same time and down the back steps running.

When they hit the landing, he said, "You get the back door, and

I'll get the front. Make sure she doesn't get outside. If you spot her, let me know and I'll approach her." Milton knew the responsibility was his, but there was something more than duty to the store in his urgent tone. There was something personal here but no one saw it at the time. No one *could* see it. Milton was moving too fast for anyone to get a good look at his eyes and the pallor of his skin.

Lois headed for the back of the store and Milton to the front. There, just as he was supposed to be was the janitor Ernest Tolley, dressed in his signature bib overalls, plaid shirt, tie, and dress hat. He turned his head with each customer who entered or exited the front doors like he was an angel guarding the Garden of Eden.

"Has she come this way, Ernest?" Milton asked, his feet never stopping.

"No, sir. I ain't seen her or I'd a nabbed her."

"Sit on her if you have to," Milton said as he walked hurriedly back through the store, checking each wide, wooden-floored aisle. But no Millie. And where was Lois and why wasn't she covering her half of the store? He was almost at the back door when he saw three figures through the glass, huddled on the sidewalk. Lois and Tiny Grant, the store's other janitor, stood on either side of Millie Franklin, holding her by the arms. Milton's palpitations were immediately cured as his heart stopped beating altogether.

Milton looked back to discover that three clerks, curious, frightened, and amazed, had followed him and were standing, staring, and waiting for his next move. It had already gone too far. At least six people knew what had happened. Heaven only knows how many customers had already picked up on the excitement and the whispers. It was too late to do anything except the right thing, the expected thing. He would have to bring her into the storeroom, call the police, and hold her until they questioned her, searched her, and arrested her.

Macalbee's had strict policies about how such matters were to be handled, which left little room for innovation. Any one of the onlookers could say the wrong word at the wrong time and the home office in Richmond would have wind of it before sun set on another day. That's how it was with a chain store. Oh, he might not get fired, of course, but Milton didn't want any negative attention to his managerial style.

Despite the name, Macalbee's Five and Dime was not a nickel-and-dime operation. It started as a family store in the state's capital nearly a quarter of a century earlier and had grown steadily throughout the South ever since. The Mt. Jefferson branch was the twenty-third to open, and Milton felt lucky to be part of such a flourishing company. And yet even in this most guarded of moments, standing here with all his employees seeing everything but his private thoughts, he had to admit to himself that Richmond and the revered Macalbee family was not the only reason he was dreading this present situation. The preacher's kid? Bad enough. But he was more concerned right now with the wrath of her mother.

Milton closed his eyes and rubbed his forehead and inhaled a deep breath that he wished had been full of Chesterfield tar and nicotine. But a cigarette would have to wait. He had some work to do.

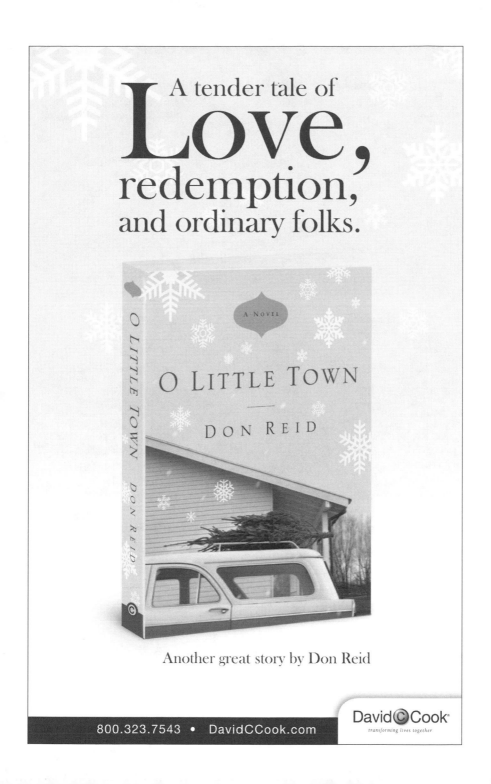